THE MACHINE IS LEARNING

Tanuj Solanki is the author of four books of fiction. His last two novels, *Manjhi's Mayhem* and *The Machine Is Learning*, were longlisted for the JCB Prize for Literature. In 2019, Solanki received the Sahitya Akademi Yuva Puraskar for his short-story collection, *Diwali in Muzaffarnagar*. His first novel, *Neon Noon*, was shortlisted for the Tata Literature Live! First Book Award in 2016. Solanki's work has been anthologised in *The Hachette Book of Indian Detective Fiction*, edited by Tarun Saint, and *A Case of Indian Marvels*, edited by David Davidar – an anthology of the works of notable Indian writers under the age of forty. Solanki's articles, short stories, and reviews have appeared in *Vogue India*, *Indian Express*, *Caravan*, *Scroll.in*, and *Hindu*, among other publications.

The Machine Is Learning was listed by the *Guardian* as among the 'Top 10 stories of modern India', and by the *Hindu* as among the 'Ten Best Fiction Books of 2020'.

Praise for *The Machine Is Learning*

'Drawing on the years he has spent in the strange world of insurance, Tanuj Solanki writes one of those rare novels which deals with the world of work, where his protagonist circles India, terminating unwanted employees and flushing his cufflinks down the toilet in an airport loo. A keenly observed and nuanced portrait of the working life, this novel tells you what it must be like to be part of the Tinder generation'

– Jerry Pinto, award-winning author of *Em and the Big Hoom* and *Murder in Mahim*

'A rare macro picture of what advancement shifts or scrapes on the sides when it takes a step forward'

– Manik Sharma, *Firstpost*

'[*The Machine is Learning*] is less about tech… and more about corporate life and the essence of being a cog in the machine. Even more brilliant is its examination of courage and indifference, and the way they intersect with class'

– Aravind Jayan, *Guardian*

'Our protagonist is an employee caught between ambition and accountability. His journey to consciousness is the heart of the story. Although he and the other characters are representatives of different world views, Solanki makes sure each is a living, breathing, individuated persona'

– Mihir Balantrapu, *Hindu*

'Solanki presents us with a coming-of-age story of the Indian who lives in a bubble. His insight into the confusion and angst of middle-class India when confronted with its own hypocrisy is reason enough to read this novel and keep it close'

– Percy Bharucha, *Hindustan Times*

'Firmly located in the realm of the modern-day corporate workplace, The Machine sets itself apart from most Indian literary novels, which continue to shy away from such a milieu [...] It's an audacious decision that could easily have given the novel its driest parts (a reminder here that we're talking about the operations of an insurance company) but it works instead as a fascinating act of world-building. And within its contours, Solanki is able to display a deep insight into [...] the intricate web of conservatism, ambition, and insecurities within which most of India's upper middle class operates'

– Harsimran Gill, *Scroll.in*

'This novel is a deep dive into the world of Artificial Intelligence and the lives of the people around it. It takes us into an algorithmic, contemporary universe, all the while shedding light on the social implications and consequences of something so overarching in our lives. Tanuj Solanki takes up the very tough task of writing in the present tense constantly and does it with ease'

– JCB Prize Jury

THE MACHINE IS LEARNING

TANUJ SOLANKI

PAN

First published 2020 by Macmillan
First published in paperback 2024 by Pan
an imprint of Pan Macmillan Publishing India Private Limited
707 Kailash Building,
26 K. G. Marg, New Delhi 110001
www.panmacmillan.co.in

Pan Macmillan, The Smithson, 6 Briset Street, Farringdon, London EC1M 5NR
Associated companies throughout the world
www.panmacmillan.com

ISBN 978-93-6113-311-4

This is a work of fiction. Names, characters, businesses, organizations, places, events, and incidents either are the product of the author's imagination or are used fictitiously. Any resemblance to actual persons, living or dead, events, or locales is entirely coincidental.

1 3 5 7 9 8 6 4 2

Typeset in Electra LT Std by R. Ajith Kumar, New Delhi
Printed and bound in India by Thomson Press India Ltd.

FSC www.fsc.org
MIX
Paper | Supporting responsible forestry
FSC® C116313

To Ashesh Solanki,
who really dislikes making software

CUFFLINKS

IT IS 11 A.M. AND THE SUN IS BRIGHT HERE IN HYDERABAD. Mitesh and I step out of the air-conditioned car and take a moment to stretch our backs. The ride from the airport took close to ninety minutes. We look sharp, though, as we ought to – shining footwear, immaculately pleated trousers, sober belt buckles, and carefully knotted blue-black ties over spotless white shirts. The shirts are pinched at the wrists in company-insignia cufflinks; each cufflink is a small silver ellipse encasing a red ***B*** on navy blue background. I tap mine for that 'official' feeling. Then I breathe in deeply and loudly, which is to convey to Mitesh how massive an improvement this roadside air is over whatever it was that we were inhaling inside the car. He laughs, shakes his head.

'A chauffeured sedan attached to you, sirs, for the whole day,' the admin folks at HO like to say, the inflection in their voices aiming to inflate our sense of entitlement. With Mitesh this works unreasonably well. The sedan gesture makes him proud even when the car is unclean and smells like a thousand years (which is to say nothing of what is done to our names on airport placards). Mitesh thinks that it signifies something that is in store for us if we do justice to the project that is currently keeping us on the road. 'The bonus this year, man…' – that's the sentence he is most fond of not finishing these days. On the flight today, as Hyderabad came into sight from his window seat, Mitesh spoke the same five words with eyes closed and eyebrows arched, as if he were having a particularly effective full-body massage.

I, on the other hand, ascribe no value to there being a sedan waiting on us everywhere. I think it means nothing. It's not like it's any real convenience either. Airport to hotel, hotel to branch office, branch office to hotel, hotel to airport – our standard lap. And this, too, only when there is an overnight stay. Otherwise, all we do is hop from airport to branch and back again. Though if you're the sort to nitpick, you would add the short drives hither-thither for lunch and dinner. But that's it. Had they not provided the car, we would have used an Ola cab and got the bills reimbursed.

'Some cities we travel to don't have those services yet,' Mitesh says whenever I bring up the Ola point. Mitesh Shah, that's his full name. A trueborn suburban-Mumbai Gujarati. Schooling (state board), graduation (B.Tech.), post-graduation (MBA) – everything in Mumbai. He is thirty-six, paunchy, balding, with a talent for producing pearls of sweat above his upper lip (temperature no concern). He has an arranged-marriage wife whose career he is not averse to calling 'a stable base'; a three-year-old boy whose exploits he is prone to recounting even without a smidgeon of interest from the counterparty; a US-settled sister whose *estate* in Nebraska he visits once every year; a long-dead mother, who he never talks about; and a recently deceased father whose death six months ago due to pancreatic cancer pushed him into buying an overpriced heart and cancer policy. Somehow, all these things – and others I don't know of – combine to make Mitesh more committed to the job, make him internalize the reality that he cannot *fuck up*, cannot *fail*, cannot *underperform*, whatever these things mean for him. As for me, I'm Saransh Malik. Born and raised in Muzaffarnagar, Uttar Pradesh, a place that I've been continuously moving away from since leaving it after school. First degree (B.Tech.) in Jaipur, second degree (MBA) in Ahmedabad. I'm twenty-nine, single, mildly heartbroken (she moved to the US about a year ago). Both parents are healthy, thank god! Parental pressure for an arranged marriage is as of now within manageable limits. Things are, generally speaking, good. But I live alone in the big city, so there are days when I wish for the sun to swallow everything. Also, days when I feel like doing surya namaskars. I guess I'm the conflicted one: too intelligent to remain in the small town, too mediocre to really change the big world. Like Mitesh, I, too, am decent at the job.

Our driver – silent throughout the drive – now jumps out of the car to help us retrieve our day-travel bags from the trunk. I notice in his long hair some badly rendered streaks of blonde. He's very young, probably in his late teens or early twenties, and so his desire for being fashionable has full legitimacy even though his bloodshot eyes betray how he barely has time for sleep. His car stinks because he lives a considerable part of his life in it. 'Lunchtime when, sir?' he asks me after placing the bags next to us. 'I'll call you,' I say. When he lingers, I give him two hundred rupees from my wallet.

'Hey, remember to claim this for me,' I tell Mitesh after the driver gets inside the car. 'Hate it when they just stand like that,' Mitesh says, twisting his face. I consider clarifying that I don't mind helping the driver with his lunch if it is the company that eventually pays for it, but then I sense some déjà vu, and also the thought sounds too convoluted in my head. So, I just say 'Yeah'.

We are facing Harmony Centre, a six-storied building on whose third floor is housed the bigger of the two Hyderabad branch offices of the Bansal Life Insurance Company (BLIC). That's our company – the establishment we grind for. Looking up at the building facade we see numerous signboards. Facing BLIC on the same floor is a branch office of one of our competitors from the life insurance industry. On the floor above us there is a stockbroking house. And on the first floor, two famous private banks' branches see eye to eye. The buildings surrounding Harmony Centre have even more direct or indirect competitors, all in the business of getting a piece of your household savings pie. This is how it happens in financial services – the providers, armed with the same data on population distribution, affluence of neighbourhoods, and property rentals, end up opening shop in the same area in any given city; soon, there is an agglomeration, which newer providers flock to simply because the area is seen as a financial hub. Over time, in order to serve the cravings and compulsions of those who come to work in these places, paan shops, tea stalls and restaurants begin to thrive.

To our left, for example, there is a small paan shop, and three salesmen – each with a cigarette in one hand and a wafer-thin plastic cup brimming with chai in another – are staring at us with the knowledge that we've come from some company's head office (our shirts and ties are more expensive than theirs, and Mitesh has his sunglasses lodged above his forehead, benignly reflecting the sun and all). Nine out of ten times head office means Mumbai, which is, of course, correct in our case.

We pull our bags inside Harmony Centre and take one of the elevators in the front lobby. It opens right opposite the BLIC branch's entrance. We face a glass door. The view through it is blocked by a poster that shows a middle-aged woman standing arms akimbo, her face radiating a ridiculous amount of confidence. 'I took the challenge and now I earn Additional Income EVERY MONTH. Can YOU do it, too?' The company wants more housewives to become insurance agents.

Life insurance branches are cramped places. Reception, customer service 'bay', waiting room, cubicles, cabins, training rooms, toilets, pantry – all jammed inside an area that is seldom more than two thousand square feet. Hyderabad-1 is no different. We push the door open and the reception is right there, three or four feet away. The receptionist is a woman of my age, seven to eight months pregnant, her hair parting loaded with an absurd amount of sindoor. What will the office do when she goes on maternity leave, I wonder. They won't hire a replacement, not on a temporary basis. It is likely that the security guard outside will double up as a receptionist. If I tell Mitesh what I'm thinking, he will actually start deliberating if including reception duties in the security guard's work brief could be looked at as a cheaper permanent solution. He's that way, steadfast in his pursuit of efficiency and effectiveness and other such things. I'm the one who observes, the one who drifts.

The receptionist makes us enter some details in a register and ushers us into a waiting room. The branch manager will reach in another ten-fifteen minutes, she tells us. Mitesh asks if she can have someone get us tea from the stall downstairs. He insists that he doesn't want the tea from the machine in the pantry. It's a weird request, for it is not that the receptionist has peons at her disposal for that kind of thing. She nods hesitantly and leaves.

The waiting room is no different from the waiting rooms in all the branch offices that we have visited in the past month. These rooms were redesigned by Marketing last year after a big brainstorming exercise the aim of which was to come up with ways to lower the percentage of customers leaving us before time, which is to say, customers surrendering their insurance policies before the completion of their term. Why does a customers do that? Well, the customer might have been provoked by a competitor who has somehow convinced them that a better financial product exists, or the customer might have encountered a sudden, genuine need for cash, or the customer might simply be motivated by any one of a million possible reasons why people sometimes just want their fucking money back. For the company, though, a policy surrender is a disastrous event. It screws up the assumptions and is bad for the bottom-line. That means it's bad for everything and everyone. Naturally, there are a lot of actions taken to curb policy surrenders. But consider the challenge: as a company, how do you dissuade the customer from doing something that is their right to do? A right that the regulator ensures you have to communicate to the customer at the time of the sale itself ? A right that, when exercised, often leads to money flowing from you to a direct competitor? Easy – you complicate the process, you make it slow, you give yourself as much time as you can to change the customer's mind. For example, BLIC doesn't allow policy surrenders to be initiated through its website. You thought you could click a few buttons and get your money back? Forget it! The customer has to visit a branch. By internal estimate, this inconvenience alone makes 23 per cent of customers enquiring about policy surrenders forgo the idea. That's money saved, money made.

For the remaining 77 per cent, it is during the branch visit that the waiting room or the 'Take a Deep Breath Room', as it is called now, plays a role. First of all, any customer seeking to surrender a policy is not heeded to immediately. A Local Operations Executive (LOE) ushers them into this room, offers tea or coffee (the pantry-machine one), and promises to ask for a senior person to handle their request. After that the customer is left to himself or herself (it's mostly himself) for at least five minutes. During this period, the artwork on the walls does its work on the customer's psyche.

So then, behold the 'Take a Deep Breath Room'. We see to our left a large picture of a family (husband, wife, two kids) with their house in the background. The house's paint and plaster have come unstuck in patches and the garden in the front is dried brown; the whole ensemble looks poor, with the children carrying tattered dolls. On the right, the same family looks perfectly hale and hearty. Now the house is perfectly painted, the garden has bursts of hibiscus, and the young boy has a tennis racquet in his hand. The difference? On the left is a family whose key decision-maker (the husband) surrendered his policy due to a temporary cash crunch. On the right is the same family when the husband decided to somehow tide over the difficult time and persisted with his policy, ultimately reaping rich rewards at the time of policy maturity. The copy accompanying the two images articulates this contrast. It's quite in-your-face if you ask me. And I'm sure it annoys a few customers. But then, it has been proven to work for quite a good number of them. More than 30 per cent of customers who spend time in this room forgo the idea of surrendering their policies.

After about ten minutes, the Branch Manager (BM) joins us. His name is Veera Reddy. He shakes our hands and sits across the round table placed in the middle of the room.

Reddy has not a single hair on his head and has thinning eyebrows that accentuate the rather unctuous totality that is his face. There is a strange round protuberance on his forehead, the mark of an old injury that looks like a button inviting to be pressed. He's dressed in a light-blue shirt and double-pleated black trousers, and I notice that he is wearing cufflinks, too, though not the company-insignia ones that we have on. His oxfords shine way more than ours, and the blue and gray socks above them (visible as he turns to my side and crosses his legs) have sharp rhombuses stretched taut over his legs. 'So, sirs, what brings you to Hyderabad?' he asks, wiping the sweat off his uneven forehead with a white handkerchief.

In terms of authority, a BM is like the CEO of a branch office, though the BM's ambit isn't as all-encompassing as a CEO's would be. That's because the cost of running a branch is taken care of by HO through strict controls on purchases and expenditures, and the BM's role is focussed on selling more insurance. The reporting lines of the entire sales staff in the branch end with the BM. The admin and operations staff, including the LOEs – people who execute all the transactions inside the branch – do not report to the BM, but to an operations hierarchy independent from sales. It is the LOEs that we want to interview today. But accessing anyone or anything inside the branch without meeting the BM is seen as an encroachment. It is a cultural thing – the BM's sovereignty over the branch is essential and to be necessarily acknowledged by *guests* from the HO. We, Mitesh and I, don't mind this ritual one bit. This bald guy sitting before us is the king of this 2,000-square-feet kingdom, and we are foreign emissaries. But he's a king who can't deny the emissaries anything. Kind of like the puppet rajas the British entertained in their India.

Responding to Reddy's question, Mitesh begins to explain like he usually does – laboriously. 'The first phase of our project is over,' he says. 'Sales teams across the country have started using iSmart – our digital application for pre-sales, quotations, form-filling and document capture – to sell insurance. Earlier, as you know, there was reliance on paper forms and attested photocopies and whatnot. And the company would have to bear the cost of couriering these forms from all across the country to a central office in Mumbai, then having them scanned, then having their data entered in our systems, and then storing the heaps and heaps of paper in a lock-and-safe environment. Now, by ensuring that our sales teams fill forms digitally and upload customer documents as photographs, the company has saved a good amount of money on the costs of managing paper flows.'

I can sense from Reddy's facial expression that an efficiency perspective, which is what Mitesh is providing, is not really having an effect. He is a sales guy, after all. For him, iSmart was a pain; all of his people had to learn how to use the app, had to fundamentally change the way they conducted their business. *Transition*, that's what they went through. And that is never fun. So I try to make it more relatable. 'iSmart has also helped sales productivity,' I say. 'Incentives have been higher this year. Earlier, your people had to carry paper brochures and printed rate charts to their customer meetings. Now, all they have to carry is their mobile phones. It's much simpler, you'd agree. The iSmart application already has all the material needed to…'

'Very happy, sirs,' Reddy says with a smile, 'I am very happy to meet the good people who made iSmart. It's a very good application. But my people have a lot of suggestions to improve it. And there are times during month-ends when the app becomes very slow.'

'We would love to have feedback from you, Veera,' Mitesh says. 'I suggest you collate the feedback from your team. What they have to say about the app… the speed and functionality, et cetera… whatever… put it together and email it to us. We'll work on it, I promise. But, actually, we aren't here for that today. We're here for the next phase of the project. And the next phase is about improving how things are done for the operations people.'

'Oh, so you want to meet Ops people?' Reddy says, somewhat relieved. Then his face becomes impassive and he looks at us for an awkwardly long time, perhaps trying to gather signs of an ulterior motive in what we've asked for. I guess right now he thinks of us as smug bastards with an all-too-important agenda up our asses. And the only way he can assert his power is by making us wait these extra seconds. For some reason, my mind's eye flashes through scenes from Hollywood movies where federal agents visit a local police station and browbeat the officers there with their superior practices. *Shit, the feds are here*, that's what the provincial police officers say in almost every movie. The feds are never a good thing for them, even if they are there to help.

'Sure,' Reddy says eventually. 'There are three people in the Ops area in Hyderabad-1. I will introduce them to you. And then you guys can take it from there?'

'Sure, that works,' says Mitesh.

Reddy opens the door and shouts for the three LOEs to come to our room. They arrive within seconds and stand in front of the dire family image, with their hands tied behind their backs. Reddy introduces us gravely, as 'important people who've come from HO on an important project in which you can all play an important part.' We stand up and shake hands with the LOEs and announce that we need forty-five minutes to an hour with each of them. We select the first interviewee at random. Reddy and the other two LOEs exit the room. Just then, the receptionist brings in the cups of tea that Mitesh had asked for. She says something about having to request a friend. I ask the interviewee if she wants tea. The receptionist's face turns stiff; in her line of work, she doesn't bring tea for the LOEs. Thankfully, the interviewee refuses, and the receptionist leaves the room.

We sit down and ask the interviewee to take a seat as well. She does so warily, coughing a couple of times. We take out our notebooks. Mitesh also produces a small booklet, our LOE Interaction & Fact Extraction (LIFE) guide. I don't like the hush in the room, so I wave my notebook to the interviewee and say, 'It's so that we don't miss anything.' She only gives a timid smile in response. She's a young woman, my age or a couple of years here and there. She has dark patches under her eyes, sunken cheeks, and looks a bit too feeble overall. She's married, I notice from the usual signs. She's dressed in a maroon salwar-kameez with a sheer white dupatta, one end of which she's now twisting around her right index finger.

I click my ballpoint pen on and scribble the date on the notebook. I write 'Hyderabad-1' next to it. Then my eyes drift and I notice the sandal on the LOE's right foot – sole split slightly near the big toe. There is chipped nail polish on the toenail; the toenail is chipped, too.

'What's your name?' I ask, looking up and making eye contact.

'Vijayalaxmi,' she answers.

'Do you mind if I take a photo?' Mitesh says, already in the process of switching on the camera app on his phone. 'It helps us to remember who we spoke to. We will be taking notes here as you see. And it helps, you know, when we go through the notes back in HO, it helps to put a face to the words.'

By the time Vijayalaxmi says 'Yes' the photo is already clicked. I have a feeling that she doesn't really understand English very well. To signal this to Mitesh, I speak my next words very slowly: 'We will ask you very simple questions. About what you do. Your daily work. OK?'

'Why…' Vijayalaxmi says, 'means… why… you ask?'

'We want to help LOEs with their work. By improving the software systems and work plans that they work with. We will make new software if needed. For that we need to understand their work, their daily activities, things like that.'

'OK.'

'So, Vijayalaxmi,' I start, 'when did you start working as LOE?'

'April of 2013, sir.'

'So about four and a half years ago. Is this your first job?'

'Yes, sir. Means… earlier I do small job. In shop. But in big company this first job.'

'What kind of shop? Your first job.'

'Jewellery shop, sir.'

Neither Mitesh nor I am noting these details down. I pause for him to ask the next question. This interchanging between us is recommended in the LIFE guide.

'Do you like it here as a LOE?' Mitesh asks, leaning in.

Vijayalaxmi smiles diffidently.

'Can you take us through your typical day?'

'Means… sir?'

'OK, let me ask you in a different way…'

Because of her inability to communicate well with us, interviewing Vijayalaxmi takes much longer than usual. By the time we are done with her it is 1 p.m. and Mitesh is hungry. I call the driver and ask him to take us to a place where we can get good biryani. The driver reveals that he is a vegetarian from UP and that he doesn't really know any good places for biryani. Undeterred, we use Google maps to take us to the nearest well-rated restaurant, a joint named Nawab. There, just after we place our orders, Mitesh gets a call from Veera, who complains about us doubting his hospitality by leaving for lunch without informing him.

Mitesh handles the situation discreetly. Sales guys can be insufferable over lunch, using us HO folks like conduits of information about their big bosses in Mumbai. We have learned to avoid them in such ostensibly informal settings, though I'm sure this distance will be difficult to keep next week when we visit Bathinda.

The biryani we have is just about all right. Like always, I pay and Mitesh keeps the receipt. This is because I am in the habit of misplacing bills. He will claim the expense and then give the money to me. He claims all my expenses.

Outside Nawab, we stand next to a paan shop and light a cigarette each. Both of us smoke the same brand, Classic Milds, but our styles of smoking are different. Mitesh exhales slowly and sometimes through the nose; I blow out the smoke through a small round vent that I create by scrunching my lips sideways.

'She was so frightened,' Mitesh says, looking at the road and the rabid traffic in front of us.

'Anyone would be,' I say. 'I mean, look at us.'

'Yeah. Do you think they can sense?'

'Sense what?'

'What we intend to do? What the company intends to do?'

'The paranoid among them, perhaps.'

'With her, I felt it somehow,' Mitesh says. 'I felt a bit strange.' He changes his hold on the cigarette – two fingers now at the top, the thumb at the bottom.

'Because she was frightened?' I ask.

'She wasn't forthcoming. Even if these LOEs can't

imagine the whole thing it must be clear to them that there is something unique happening. No one has ever come from the HO to talk to them. Ever. They must chat about this amongst themselves. Maybe they have a WhatsApp group where they do this sort of thing, a community of LOEs.'

'That's possible. But is that a problem?'

'No, I guess not. Even if some of them had suspicions what could they do?'

'How about we assign them a new, arbitrary task. Some sort of silly diktat so that they gossip about HO's stupidity instead of speculating about the interviews,' I say.

'That's a good idea,' says Mitesh, 'in fact, that's a spectacular idea.'

'What will you do without me?' I say.

We laugh. Mitesh drops his cigarette stub, squishing it under his shoe just to make sure. I pull two greedy drags and then do the same. I feel a bit dyspeptic; it's the heat or the biryani. I loosen my tie a bit, take off the cufflinks, put them in my trousers' pocket, and roll up my sleeves.

We re-enter the branch at about 2:30 p.m. and find the 'Take a Deep Breath Room' occupied by a customer. 'Surrender request,' the LOE we are to interview next tells us with a sly smile. He knows the conspiratorial aspect of retaining a surrendering customer; knows that all of HO's messaging – how 'Surrenders are BAD for the customer', or how 'by stopping surrenders, we create VALUE for EVERYONE' – is dissimulation. Then there is the joy of knowing that he is on the right side of an instance of information asymmetry. The surrendering customer knows less than him, and in the well-rehearsed drama that plays out in the 'Take a Deep Breath Room', the LOE is in a position of pleasurable power; just like how it is a source of pleasure to us that we know more about the purpose of the interaction that we are to have with him – his name is Chandrasekhar – than he does.

For the interview, Chandrasekhar leads us into the Ops room. On one side, the room has a glass panel affixed with two round speakers in the middle and two rectangular openings at the bottom. Through the openings, sales guys and customers on the other side pass in insurance application forms, documents, cheques, cash, et cetera to the LOEs manning the counters. The LOEs' broad job description is to check if everything passed to them is good-to-process, to punch in some identifying information in a couple of software systems, and to put any paper documents or payment instruments that they receive in their respective *outward* trays. Of course, for iSmart cases, since everything is digital, there is nothing received from anyone and nothing to be *outwarded*.

There are 552 LOEs in the company, across 224 branch locations. But what the LOEs actually do is a thing only superficially known. Over the years, as business processes have grown more complex – the addition of new distribution channels, constantly changing regulations, ever-innovative insurance frauds – the LOE role has become complex too. This means that while the general rules of their work are known, the exceptions are not; and that the exceptions have increased in number. The upshot is that every LOE today has enough leeway to act as per their own interpretation, especially in situations about which they have received no formal guidance. In HO-speak: 'localized rule sets have organically sprung up for managing exceptions.' In easy-speak: 'the LOEs have put their brains where HO didn't.' Of course, none of the local know-how is coded or standardized, which has led to high dependence on individuals. We know of many LOEs who have become so important to their branches that all activity ceases on days when they are on leave. For long, HO's response to such slow seepage in control has been to be a bit generous with regards to their salary increments and bonuses, making the LOE role the best paid among the lowest-paid roles in the company (for perspective: I make twelve times an average LOE; the CEO about sixty times). The only grouse LOEs have is that their bonuses seem randomly distributed. This is simply because HO doesn't know how to measure LOE performance. Batting in the dark, many senior people in HO routinely express suspicions about LOEs shirking work, something that I have seen no evidence of. The HO insecurity is real, though, germinating from a situation where the LOEs execute all the operations inside a branch, but to HO it remains a mystery as to what they do on an hour-by-hour basis. It's not the LOEs' fault, of course; they have made no conscious or concerted effort to bring about this situation. It's just the way things have turned out to be over the years.

Arguably, it is for blessed codification that Mitesh and I – federal agents, so to speak – are interviewing LOEs across different branches in the country. But we have no intention of documenting standards or making a comprehensive mega-manual. Nothing that we produce will go back to the LOEs as help. In fact, what we produce will not be used by a single LOE. That's the information asymmetry whose bright side we bask in.

Inside the Ops room now, we are joined by Vijayalaxmi and the other LOE. The two of them proceed to man the transaction counter. On the other side of the counter, a customer turns up with an address-change request. As I take out my notebook, Mitesh nudges my elbow. 'We can't do the interview here. The LOEs have to be interviewed alone,' he says, tapping the LIFE guide.

'It's all right,' I say.

'No,' says Mitesh.

'Is there a vacant room?' I turn to ask Chandrasekhar.

'Yes, sir,' Chandrasekhar says, 'There is a training room which must be empty now.'

We pick up our stuff to move to the available room. As I close the Ops room door on my way out, I catch Vijayalaxmi turned 180 degrees on her revolving chair, looking at me. I smile at her professionally; she only blinks in response. She's curious, I guess, but then it's not every day that people from HO visit the branch.

In the training room, we conduct the two interviews back-to-back. We learn that there are differences in how the two LOEs handle one very specific scenario: an existing female customer buying her second policy, whereby her marital status (and thus her second name) has changed in between the two purchases. A single Sheetal Gupta becoming a married Sheetal Singh. It seems natural that we should use the new information to update our existing records, that 'Sheetal Singh' should be stored in our systems. The question is: when Sheetal Singh's insurance proposal comes to the branch for receipting and our system throws up a suggestive match with Sheetal Gupta's record, should the update be made immediately, or should Sheetal's explicit *Consent & Confirmation* be sought? On the surface, it's an inane, bureaucratic issue. On a larger scale, though, the accumulation of such anomalies – a difference in the way two LOEs handle the same scenario – defeat all codification efforts. It is such anomalies that we are here to find (not a mere exception, but an exception that is handled differently by different people). We realize from the interviews that while Chandrasekhar insists on this written *Consent & Confirmation* before receipting the fresh case, Raja, the other LOE, does not. Raja just updates the name directly, making the assumption that by providing documents carrying her latest name the woman has implicitly consented to an update of details in our records.

After we are done with the interviews – which is around 4:30 p.m. – we reach out to Veera Reddy in the BM's cabin and deliver our goodbyes. He says he hopes that we have given the LOEs some good sense. 'Sometimes they just arbitrarily deny salespeople,' he complains. 'It impacts the business.'

Mitesh, armed with the discovery of the day, is now favourably disposed to agree with anything said about the arbitrariness of LOEs. 'Yes, Veera, we have taken notes. We will work on it.'

We have a quick tea session with Reddy after which we express our desire to beat the traffic and reach the airport early. Reddy saves our phone numbers and vows to reach out to us the next time he's in Mumbai. We leave his room and walk towards the branch exit.

On our way out I see the Ops area window from the other side. Vijayalaxmi, behind the glass now, is dealing with an impatient salesperson tapping his knuckles on the counter. She says something to him and peers into the computer screen in front of her. From the way her eyes are switching between the two halves of the screen (like a video gamer's), I deduce that she is matching the details on the digital form (on the left half of the screen) against the corresponding documents provided as images (on the right half of the screen). This step, known as *scrutiny*, is necessary before accepting the application and giving the salesperson what he wants, which is nothing but a receipt of the case – usable as proof before his boss that he brought in business during the day. Scrutiny is the step where errors of judgment and errors of oversight can happen. And scrutiny is, among others, a task that we now have the technology to automate.

We didn't discuss with Vijayalaxmi the married-woman scenario that we did with the other two LOEs. Not very *standardized* of us, I think. The contradiction makes me smile to myself. If I tell Mitesh, he will likely give me a spiel about how the same rules cannot apply to those who are managers and those who are part of the general workforce. Or he will just show me the LIFE guide. Either way, he will take the joy out of my observation.

We take the elevator down and step outside Harmony Center. I call the driver, who informs me that he is going to have to take a U-turn from further up the road to be on our side. Forced to wait, we proceed to buy cigarettes from the paan shop. As I light my cigarette, I hear my name being called in an awkward way. I look back to find it's Vijayalaxmi.

'Sir… Saransh sir,' she says.

'Yes?'

'Sir, I… Give me phone number sir… your please.'

'You want my phone number?' I look at Mitesh, who is exhaling smoke the only way he knows.

'Yes, sir.'

'Why do you want it?'

'Just, sir… I… help.'

'OK, OK.' I recite my number as she types and stores it in her phone. Then she says 'thanks' to me and walks back to the building.

'The beginning of a cross-cultural romance,' Mitesh quips.

'Fuck off,' I say, though I am seriously wondering just what a LOE might want my number for.

The car pulls up in front of us. I signal to the driver to wait till we finish our cigarettes. Once inside the car, Mitesh asks for my notebook so that he can compare our observations. To me, this exercise is overkill. But Mitesh never considers the day's work over until we have gone through the notes again and improved them if need be.

I get a call from George, our colleague from the HO, who, as it happens, is on a branch visit to Lucknow. Ankita, another colleague, is accompanying George. I put the phone on speaker. George asks about our day. I tell him how uneventful it was, but I'm corrected by Mitesh, who details, not without delight, the anomaly we discovered in Hyderabad-1. George answers in a series of 'oh kays', after which he provides details of the anomaly that he discovered in Lucknow. I'm switched off from the conversation to really heed what he's saying. That's no problem though – there will be enough time to learn about all the anomalies.

When we reach the airport the driver lingers mutely again after helping us with our luggage. This time we show no generosity. After check-in and security, we dash towards the first bar that hovers into view. Once there, we waste no time in asking for Budweiser pints and some fries. There is a TV not very far from our table; *Terminator II* is playing on the screen. 'Such a simple story,' Mitesh says during the truck-chase sequence in which Schwarzenegger flip-cocks his shotgun multiple times. 'The future doesn't wear leather jackets, it wears cufflinks,' I say prophetically, or perhaps absent-mindedly. Mitesh reacts with a 'Huh?' After half a minute he adds, 'I'm the only one wearing them now.' This little joke is the only conversation we have in the bar.

After the third pint, Mitesh signals his desire to stop and I call for the check. We split the bill on our debit cards – the company doesn't pay for alcohol on trips. We move from the bar to the gate from where we are to board the aircraft. I need to use the toilet, so I tell Mitesh to keep a watch over my bags.

It is on my way to the toilet that it occurs to me that I haven't checked Facebook the entire day. Once I've found an empty stall and taken my perch, so to speak, I flick open my phone to fall into the distractions that the medium offers. While looking through my feed I find something strange: five people have shared identical Facebook memories, calling for fresh outrage and grief over a news item from exactly two years ago: a three-year-old Syrian boy, drowned, his body washed up on the Turkish coast. I vaguely remember this event from when it happened as the fallout of something far too distant from my life. Out of curiosity, I click on one of the posts. There are two pictures.

The first one shows the boy's body on the beach – clothes drenched in sea-water, face against the sand, small palms looking up to the sky. His knees are bent, his hips raised. Save for the positioning of the palms, he looks like – or perhaps I now want him to look like – an overexcited child having a great day at the beach, a child who's just tripped over himself and fallen face-first on the sand. And it is as if the precise moment in which his face hit the sand has been captured by a photographer, who could very well be his father. And even though the child is hurt by the fall, he will stand up gingerly the very next second, stifle a sob, and look guiltily at his parents. And then the mother will lovingly scold him while patting the sand off his clothes. And as soon as he's clean enough the child will free himself from her grip and dash off to make his sandcastles or whatever, for it is not every day that his parents bring him to the beach.

But none of this will be true. His palms are not in front of his head, not facing down like they would have if he had fallen – they are aligned to his lifeless torso and open upwards. The child is dead. Drowned.

The second picture shows a Turkish police officer carrying the body. Only the child's legs are visible in this one. The officer can see the child's face if he wants to, but in the photo hc seems to be consciously looking away. He doesn't want to be haunted by the face, I think. It is also possible that the officer avoids the child's face because he feels guilty – guilty of being an adult in a world where a child can die the way this one has.

I read the text that accompanies the news item and learn the boy's name. Alan Kurdi. *Alan Kurdi*, I whisper, almost involuntarily. Then, in the very next moment, I realize how incredibly important an illusion of anonymity is. Because taking the child's name has changed everything. Now the name and its unknowable story are committed to my memory. Now the images are burnt in my mind even more sharply.

I blink hard, sniffle, finish my downstairs business. After I stand up, I notice something that befits nothing, least of all this moment: my company-insignia cufflinks are in the commode! They must have slipped out of my pocket when I pulled up my pants, I reason. I can't make myself pick them up, of course. So I do the only thing I can do. I flush. Two red Bs in silver ellipses swirl with shit and water and are sucked into the beyond.

SCRABBLE

SATURDAY MORNING. I WAKE UP AND OF COURSE THE FIRST thing I do is look into my phone. Nothing significant there, except a new message on WhatsApp. It is from the woman I had matched with on Tinder about a week before the trip to Hyderabad. Jyoti – that's her name. She sent me a 'Hi' a few minutes after 1 a.m. last night, which probably makes it a drunk-and-lonely 'Hi'. I get out of bed thinking I should just ignore it. I feel a slight headache, maybe due to the six Budweiser pints that I had last night in the company of a passive-aggressive friend, someone who works in a small-time advertising firm and is so envious of me for earning more than him that he spends half of our time together in trying to locate a scam in my Muzaffarnagar-to-Mumbai story. Feeling the slight pounding in my temples, I curse him loudly as I stumble to the kitchen to make myself a cup of tea.

In the kitchen, while the tea brews, I swipe open my phone and stare at the 'Hi' again. I convince myself that it is rude to ignore such a message, and finally, after I have poured tea into my cup, respond with a 'Hello there'. I don't expect an immediate answer; she's probably still asleep. Excited anyway, I visit her Tinder profile wanting to affirm what exactly had made me swipe right in the first place.

There are four photographs in Jyoti's Tinder profile and all of them portray her as someone who never bothers much about being clicked. Not that she looks bad in any of them, that's not the case at all. But in each picture one can sense some sort of haste, as if there was no time to get photographed or no time to consider how the snap could be made better. It is something that I now find oddly likeable, though it's difficult to say if the effect is created by any peculiarity in her features or by the ineptitude of the person clicking the pictures (none of them are selfies). She carries a distracted expression in all her photos. Her hair is always loose, and in the main photo – the one I must have swiped right on – it is cut smartly till just above her shoulders. In this photo she is seated outdoors, the glow on her face suggesting a light source outside the frame, probably an evening bonfire. She is wearing a white pullover over a pair of blue jeans and smiling at something, a joke, perhaps – a joke that I imagine to be neither hilarious nor pathetic. Her gaze is turned sideways, probably directed at the person who cracked the joke. The fact that, apart from her, no other detail of note is discernible marks the act of taking this picture as both voyeuristic and melancholic. If I had to guess, I would say it was clicked by a boyfriend who knew he was about to lose her. But of course, I could be entirely wrong. It may just have been a photograph of a larger group, deftly cropped into a portrait after she realized she looked rather beautiful in it. Anyway, this is how you lose her, brother: she puts the picture on Tinder, and a dude far away gapes at it while sipping morning tea.

Her bio introduces her as *Ex-journalist | Do-gooder | Working on a children's book*, and as I read this description I conclude that she's cool, as I probably did the first time when I came across her profile.

We had shifted to WhatsApp soon after matching on Tinder. Her WhatsApp display picture is a beautiful sketch of a banyan tree ('Yes, it's mine… I made it,' she told me after I asked). Up till now we have made two unsuccessful attempts to set up a date. She has even given me her address and doesn't seem to mind the idea of us meeting at her place. She lives in Goregaon West, not very far from where I live.

I finish my tea and remind myself that even though our chats have been somewhat flirtatious, there is no way to be sure if there will be any progress. It's likely that the late-night 'Hi' was a mistake or, worse, that it was meant for someone else. I visit my own Tinder profile to try and see myself like Jyoti may have first seen me. My profile description causes me to suffer a not-at-all-small surge of embarrassment: *Fintech dude and peanut butter enthusiast. I will massage your head if you ask nicely.* Peanut butter!? Massage!? I spend a whole minute wondering what to change it to but then decide to keep it. Who knows what works and what doesn't?

I swipe right and left on a few more profiles just to pass the time, just to get Jyoti out of my mind, just to compensate – through dissipation – for the attention that I've already paid her. But inside five minutes of this game I feel bored, even a bit sad. It's Saturday morning and Tinder is where I am. That feels wrong. I consider reading a book. That seems too tough a thing to do. Duly I open Twitter and start scrolling in search of something to pay attention to, partly aware of the paradox implicit in the act, for my intention is mostly to file away, through the flicking motion of my thumb, my very capacity for paying attention.

Then I get a message on WhatsApp.

From Jyoti.

'How good a Scrabble player are you?'

I type 'I've long considered myself the greatest ever,' and hit send.

'We must rectify that misconception,' she says.

It is she who will come to my place, which is a bit surprising if you ask me. Women don't normally do that in the first meeting, do they? She said she'll be here around 4 p.m. That's fine by me, for it is only 11 a.m. right now and I have more than enough time to clean up the extraordinary mess that is my apartment. I live in a 1-BHK, fully-furnished, about six hundred square feet in area. I do avail the services of a bai, but she happens to be on an indefinite leave since her husband suffered a heart attack last week.

To begin with I brush the dust off the bookshelf in the living room. I own about five dozen books. More than half of them are fiction, with Russian classics and Latin American magical realists making a significant chunk. Most of the other books are about topics like techno-positivity, the oncoming AI boom, theories on social media virality, combating climate change through technology, et cetera. I've never read any of this stuff but I feel I'm someone who should be reading this stuff. When I'm done dusting, I regard the bookshelf as a whole and, anticipating Jyoti's taste – even though I have no way of doing so – change the order of books a bit, putting topical conversation starters in more prominent places.

I then change my dirty pillow covers and bed sheets and move all my unwashed laundry into the bag nominally assigned to it. After that, as I clean my commode with Harpic, I allow myself the thought that even if the only outcome of the rendezvous with Jyoti is to be this preparation, this little shake-up from inertia, I should still count it as a positive thing.

Then there is a shower, an eggs-and-toast breakfast, and ennui. I am on my bed with a book in my hand. It's a few minutes past noon and the room is lit through the glass window on one side. The book I have started reading is a book of essays written by a woman who either wants to be or has become a tree. In her initial essays the author makes it clear that she does not like *human time* – its demands, its compressions, the whirlwinds of motion it engenders. Trees, she finds, are free of the notion of speed, which is also the kind of freedom that she seeks. At one point, my concentration breaks and I note some specifics in the ambient noise – an autorickshaw honking, a child crying, a pressure cooker whistling. I realize that I disagree with the author – I don't ever want to become a tree. If anything, we need to save human time. We need to save human time instead of fantasizing about becoming a tree.

Thinking of ways to save human time, I doze off. Like a log, for several hours.

When I wake up I find myself covered in sweat. There is no electricity! I am confused, for if this is a power cut then it is the very first one that I've experienced in my five-and-a-half years in Mumbai. I wait for about twenty minutes for the power to return then decide to ask my neighbour, who is also my landlord, if there is a power cut in his house as well. Outside his door, I press the bell which, to my surprise, makes a shrill sound. I have my answer, but when the landlord opens the door, I have to say something.

'Sorry… I… I was just checking if there is electricity in your house.'

The landlord, irritated, scrunches his thick eyebrows and caresses his tummy with his right hand. He is in his shorts and nothing else. It looks like I woke him up from a deep sleep. 'The bell rang, no?' he says.

'Yes. But there is no electricity in my house.'

'Hmm… call the electrician,' he says, and moves to close his door.

Back in my apartment, I realize that it is ten minutes past 3 and that Jyoti will be here in less than an hour. Luckily my phone has enough battery, but I don't know any electricians in the neighbourhood and don't have any number to call. I search online and find a few listings. I call the first number; nobody picks up. I dial another number and the guy tells me that he is on a service call somewhere, repairing a ceiling fan. The third one tells a similar story. This doesn't look very promising.

It's getting stuffy inside the living room so I open the window. The sky is heavy with dark clouds and it seems that it will rain. It's September, and these are the last throes of the monsoon. The incremental darkness in the room and the anticipation that Jyoti will be here soon make me panic a bit. I step out of the apartment, climb down the stairs and walk to the market nearby. I ask a couple of general store owners if they know any electricians operating in the area. They don't. Just then Jyoti calls me.

'Hey… Saibaba Complex, right?'

'Yes, Saibaba Complex.'

'Sounds like a psychological disorder,' she says.

'What?' I laugh.

'Umm… I miscalculated. I think I'm really close to your Saibaba Complex.'

'OK.'

'Actually, I'll reach in another ten minutes. Is that fine?'

'Oh yes, that's fine. No problem.'

'Cool. See you.'

She disconnects the call. I remember that I don't have any condoms in the house. I buy a pack. There is nothing to be done about the power cut now. I feel hassled, so I buy a pack of cigarettes and light one up.

When I hear a knock on the door, my immediate reaction is to rush to the bathroom and check my appearance in the mirror. Closely-cropped hair, a greenish one-day stubble, brown eyes, a high forehead, a sharp nose… I think I'm all right. I am wearing a plain gray T-shirt and a pair of light-green shorts. Casual, but that's the play.

I hold the door open, and a long 'Hey' comes out of my mouth as if I'm meeting an old friend. 'Your doorbell doesn't ring?' – these are Jyoti's first words, muttered as if to herself. She takes a moment to wipe her sandals on the doormat. She's wearing a frilly brown shirt and a pair of tight black jeans. Her hair is tied in a ponytail. From her left shoulder hangs a faux-leather bag, jutting from which is a black umbrella and a Scrabble box wrapped in transparent polythene. Clearly, the box has never been opened, which makes me entertain the thought that she bought it only today, probably on her way here. Which suggests that in the morning she had talked of Scrabble just to talk of something, to create some pretense for meeting me.

'Water?' I ask while gesturing her to sit on the sofa.

'Yes, please,' she sits down.

I give her a glass of water from the refrigerator. 'Umm… actually, there is no electricity.'

'Yeah, I was wondering why it's so dark in here,' she says, her eyebrows raised in confusion. She gulps down the water. Her eyebrows are immaculate.

'Yeah. It just went off and I haven't been able to find an electrician.'

'Oh.'

I slide the living room's window completely open. 'It's raining now, will be cooler at least,' I say. Clearly, this hasn't begun well. 'You want anything else? Tea? Beer? Anything to eat?'

'Yeah, beer will be good,' Jyoti says.

She removes her hair tie and lets her hair loose and runs her fingers through it a few times. The sky outside rumbles. I take two cans of Budweiser from the fridge and pass one to her. Then I sit down on the sofa, two cushion-lengths away from her, and twiddle my thumbs.

'So,' she says, 'should we start?'

'Sure.'

Jyoti unwraps the Scrabble box and hands over the polythene to me, which I dump in the dustbin in the kitchen. We pull the centre table towards the sofa and lay the board on it. We take seven letter tiles each from a translucent bag. 'Hope you're ready, 'cause I'm going to kick your ass,' says Jyoti, and given how awkward the electricity situation has made this first meeting of ours, I am at the moment grateful for any competitiveness she can muster, anything that can serve as a distraction. Nothing else will happen today, I already know that in my gut.

After five or six turns, it becomes clear that Jyoti is better at this than I am. Not necessarily because of having a superior vocabulary, but because of having played the game more often than I have. She doesn't care about making a lengthy word at each turn but maximizing her score. She has an eye for prefixing or suffixing my words and consuming a double-word or a triple-word slot, eventually making more points with the extension than I do with the original. Basically, I am getting my ass kicked. Which is also why I get excited when I extract a blank tile from the bag.

D Q U K _ I P

The word I have in my head is QUICK, with the blank used as a C. But there is no letter in its spelling that is available on the board, so there is nowhere to place QUICK. There is a bare A with open space to its left and right. I drop the QUICK idea and think of using the blank as a consonant other than C. I try out different ones in my head using the available A. After discarding some options, I think of the blank as an R, and as soon as I do that, the letters from my pack reassemble in my mind's eye to form a word on their own.

KURDI.

The KURDI of Alan Kurdi, the drowned Syrian child.

His face flat against the sand. The palms facing the sky.

The room constricts. Its air thickens. A roaring rain begins to fall.

Jyoti senses the shift perhaps. 'Hey, what's wrong?' she asks.

Unsure if the association in my mind – and its choking power – can be communicated to someone I'm meeting for the first time, I feign a mini fit of coughing and rush to the bathroom. I wash my face. As I look into the mirror above the washbasin I have the sense that I'm looking not at myself but at an approximation. I bare my teeth to the approximation. My canines look larger than usual. I take a couple of deep breaths, and it is only when Jyoti says 'Are you all right?' from the living room that I realize that I am being weird. I say 'Yeah' and wipe my face with a towel. Then I return to the living room. It seems darker than before.

'What happened?' Jyoti asks.

'Nothing. I'm sorry.'

'It looks really apocalyptic right now,' she says, pointing to the view outside the window.

'Yes.'

'The rain sounds like it will never stop.'

'Yes.'

'It's your turn.'

'Just give me a minute.'

'You know you're creeping me out a bit, right now? You are. Please don't creep me out.' She laughs nervously as she says this.

I look into her eyes and try to smile. 'I'm sorry,' I say. I sit on the sofa and look at my letters and decide to keep the blank unused. I place the word PAID on the board.

'Do you want me to leave?' Jyoti says.

'No. I don't,' I say.

'It's OK if you want to. There is no electricity. It's getting dark inside. I guess it was a stupid idea to play Scrabble anyway. Actually, I'm sorry, I shouldn't have done this.'

'I'm sorry about the light. Really. Do you want more beer? Something to eat?'

'No, Saransh. Thanks.'

'So… you want to leave because I have no electricity?' I ask.

'I can't deny that,' she says with a brief smile.

'Well, that's awkward. It's raining hard now, true.'

'Don't worry. I'll manage.'

There is silence after that, a silence in which I wonder if I should, in fact, tell her of Alan Kurdi. But what will I tell her?

'Well then, I guess I should be leaving,' she says.

'Let me come with you,' I say. 'I'll help you find an auto.'

'There is no need.'

'Please.'

Jyoti picks up her stuff, I take my umbrella and the flat's keys, and we move downstairs. It's raining heavily, perhaps for the last time this season. As we walk towards the main road, I take the time to assess what has just transpired. Jyoti must be really into me, for otherwise, she would not have come to my house with the pretense of playing Scrabble. The awkward electricity situation and the abrupt termination of the game must have made her feel unsure about me. The electricity situation cannot be helped but perhaps I can tell her about Alan Kurdi.

'I'm sorry if I scared you,' I say. We are both under our umbrellas, waiting for a vacant auto to turn up, something that becomes more unpredictable on this road whenever it's raining. 'It's just… something happened.'

'Hmm… something happened to you?' Jyoti asks.

'No. Not to me.'

'To someone close to you?'

'No. I… I don't know how to explain this.'

'It's OK if you don't want to share,' Jyoti says.

'It's not that. Well… have you seen that image… of that drowned Syrian kid?'

'That kid on the beach? Yes, who hasn't. That was a couple of years ago, no?'

'Yeah. Do you know his name?' I ask.

'His name? It was everywhere then, but I don't remember it now.'

'Alan Kurdi. That's his name.'

'Oh, yes, that was the name.'

'The letters I had on my panel,' I say, 'my letters… they were making the word Kurdi.'

She gives me a quizzical look. I can see that her interest in this conversation has suddenly increased.

'The word made me think of that image. Of him lying there on the sand. Dead. It…'

'You felt sad?'

'Aaa…'

A Toyota Innova whooshes past splashing dirty water that almost reaches us. 'Shit,' Jyoti says. Then she looks at me, 'Sorry, you were saying.'

'I don't know what I felt.'

Jyoti juts out her lower lip and nods slightly. I can't figure out what impact this is having on her.

'Look,' I say. 'I'm sorry how the afternoon turned out. But I would like us to meet again.'

'Yes, me too,' she says and smiles. 'It's just that your room is too gloomy right now. You should get an electrician before it's night. You know, if you leave the windows open the mosquitoes will definitely airlift you to a neighbouring country.

I laugh. 'Yeah, yeah, I know.'

'Do you think of that boy often?'

'No, I… I just happened to see his… the pictures of his death… I don't know what else to call them… I happened to see the pictures recently.'

'Hmm.'

We stay silent for the next two minutes. There is still no auto in sight. 'You don't have to stand here with me, Saransh,' Jyoti says.

'No, it's fine.'

'No, please. I'll be fine. In fact, I'll just call an Ola.' She takes out her cellphone and fixes one. 'See, it's going to come,' she shows me. The cab is just four minutes away. 'You can go now.'

'Sure?'

'Yep.'

'OK, then. I guess I will see you again.'

'Yes, pakka.'

'I'll make it better next time. I promise.'

'Cool.'

I give her a tentative hug, of the sideways kind, such that it is our umbrellas that have more contact with each other than us. Then I rush towards my building with conflicting feelings about this rendezvous. It is quite possible that we never see each other again.

As I enter my building, I notice the area under the staircase to my right. There are the electric meters and other electrical paraphernalia with many tiny green and red lights blinking. I pass this nook every day but it is the first time that I am really *looking* at it. The bill used to turn up at the doorstep, so it was never important for me to know where the meters were located. Now I know. I take a step closer and find the box marked with my flat's number on it: C 14. There are no lights blinking on the meter. I open the box. Inside, I notice an MCB switch that is turned downward. I turn it up. A green light begins to blink in the meter. I realize that this might have been all that was wrong with the electricity. I run up the four flights of stairs to my apartment and ring the doorbell. It works!

The very next thing on my mind is Jyoti. I climb down, taking two-three steps at a time, and walk out to the street without my umbrella. I run towards where I had left her, hoping that her Ola hasn't arrived yet. The rain doesn't take any time in drenching me. When I am about twenty metres away from Jyoti, I call her name out loud. She looks at me and gestures a question.

'The light, the light,' I shout from across the road. Just then her Ola nears. I cross the road and ask her to cancel it.

'What?' she asks.

'I found the fault. It's fixed. The light is on at my place now.'

'Really?'

'Yes, yes, please come.'

'But…'

'I want you to come, please. Let's have another beer.'

She shrugs, raising her eyebrows in mild amusement. Then she apologizes to the Ola driver, who mutters something obscene but surrenders to his fate anyway. We start walking towards my building.

We take a beer each and spread the Scrabble board again. I tell Jyoti how in Muzaffarnagar, where I grew up, there used to be two scheduled power cuts during the day. From 9 a.m. to 11 a.m., and from 2 p.m. to 5:30 p.m. 'If there was ever a few minutes' delay in a scheduled outage, those extra minutes of electricity were the equal of pure joy,' I say, 'as if those moments had been salvaged… you know… as if the monster had forgotten about its daily ransom.'

Jyoti tells me that she was born and raised in Mumbai, and for that reason has rarely seen power cuts, scheduled or random. 'But if all the homeless people were given homes,' she adds, 'which is something that absolutely must happen… then I don't know… I don't know if Mumbai will have enough power then.'

After two or three rounds of Scrabble, in which I reassert my inferiority, she rises from the sofa and walks towards the bookshelf. 'All these upbeat books, eh?' she asks. 'Seems there is nothing for the world to do but become better.'

'I hid the novels this morning, you'll find them behind the first row,' I say, candour coming easily to me now.

'Wrong move, I must say,' Jyoti says while picking up a book about how being generous at the workplace is a good strategy. 'So what exactly is it that you do, fintech dude?'

'You remember that?'

'Of course. Though I like the head massage part better.' She places the book back from where she took it and walks back to the sofa. 'Let's stop the stupid game,' she says.

'And what does an ex-journalist mean?' I say, putting the letters back in their translucent bag and folding the board.

'Someone who loves journalism too much to root for the kind that sells these days,' Jyoti says.

'What kind sells these days?'

'The scared kind,' she says. 'Or the scary kind. I don't know.'

I am at a loss to find the right words in response: what Jyoti has said seems too true and important and banal. The moment is short-lived, though, for Jyoti then poses a question that shifts the conversation to a new zone: 'So tell me, how available are you?'

It makes me heat up in the ears. I still manage to turn it into a joke: 'For the head massage?'

'That too, I guess,' Jyoti says. 'Look, I broke up with a boyfriend a few months ago. It was tough, the break-up, even though it was me calling the shots most of the time.

Or, well, I don't know. Took me some time to get over it. To be able to say that I am past it. For what? Well, I don't know. For anything. Just sex, just friendship, friendship with benefits, and other combinations as and when they suit the other party. Basically, what I'm trying to say is that I'm available.'

I nod slowly, as if considering what she's just said, though I can hear my heartbeat at this moment. 'My story is similar to yours,' I say, clearing my throat once. 'Broke up almost a year ago. And yes, available for the whole spectrum.'

'See, you're good-looking and all. I'll say that's broadly why I came to your house. And when I was leaving… the first time… when I said I wanted to meet you again, trust me I wasn't lying. It may sound weird, but that's because of that Syrian child you talked about. That comforted me. Otherwise, in here, you had me totally creeped out with your dark room and horrible Scrabble skills and your suddenly glassy eyes. Fuck, sorry, I guess I shouldn't speak like – '

'No issues there,' I say. 'You're candid, and that's something I like.'

'Do you find me attractive?' she asks.

I swallow some spit. 'Absolutely,' I say, looking straight into her eyes. 'More than attractive, yes.'

Jyoti stares right back at me. There is a mischievous look on her face. 'We can start with a kiss, then,' she proffers.

We make out on the sofa for a few minutes and then decide to move to the bedroom. Our entry there is accompanied by a clap of thunder that could not have been better-timed. I find myself on the verge of giggling but manage to hold it back. Without sharing a word, we find ourselves on the bed, on our knees, facing each other. We move closer to kiss again. I place my hands on her waist and slide them up her body. I take off her shirt. She removes my T-shirt. Her skin is darker than mine, which is something new and exciting for me. The bulge in my shorts is visible. She places her palm on it and caresses the hardness. Apart from our breathing, all we hear is the loud static of rain. We kiss again, sloppier this time, and tumble to our sides, hungry for more.

'How do you like it?' I ask her, as a nervous laugh finds a way out of me. 'Nor-mally,' she says with an amused expression. 'Sure,' I say, but the word comes out all wrong from my mouth, as if I am saying it to someone at work. She ignores it.

After some *nor-mally*, Jyoti suggests that we change positions. We shift to doggie. Within seconds our movements pick up speed. But just as our pleasure begins to increase, just as our sounds begin to turn animalistic, my phone begins to ring. Almost as a reflex, I stop and pull out a bit. Jyoti grunts and, wanting me to keep on, extends her right hand back to hold me. But I can't keep on. I kiss her back and her neck, then reach out to the phone on our right side. It is from an unknown number. 'Fucking shit,' I say, and turn the phone silent.

'Oh, for fuck's sake… pick it up now, dude,' Jyoti says in annoyance.

I do that.

'Hello? Sir?' I hear from the other end.

'Who's this?'

'Saransh sir?'

'Yes. Who is this?'

'Saransh sir. This is Vijayalaxmi, sir.'

'Who?'

'Vijayalaxmi.'

'Vijayalaxmi?'

'I take number, sir. In Hyderabad.'

'Yes, I know, I know. Why are you calling me on the weekend?'

'OK, sir. I call you Monday?'

'Yes. Call me Monday.'

'OK, sorry sir. Actually, branch open today. I forget. Sorry, sir.'

I disconnect the phone and look at Jyoti. She has shifted from her all-fours position and has her back rested on the headboard. I fear that she's angry, that the sex won't resume now.

'You're compulsive about the phone,' she says.

I scratch my head in response.

'You will need to apologize for this,' she says, touching my balls with her right foot.

I take this as a clue and go down on her.

The wake-up sex on Sunday is our fourth time. When I get up to make tea, Jyoti asks if I have spare shorts and a T-shirt that she can wear. The request stirs me, for it conveys that she intends to stay longer. Her manner is unpredictable, different from any woman that I have ever met. She walks through my apartment as if she owns it, as if there is nothing untoward in having sex and staying over after a first date (maybe there isn't). She even opens the door to pick up the Sunday paper.

We read the paper while drinking tea, and I cannot escape the thought that if a third person was watching us, he or she would not have guessed that we first met only the evening before. This fact is both awkward and thrilling for me. From her sheer nonchalance, though, it is clear that it is neither for Jyoti.

'What kind of place do you work in, again?' she asks me while peering into the paper.

'A life insurance company,' I say.

'Ah,' she says, and then shows me a news article. It contains a list of insurance companies, in descending order of the fines that were imposed on them by the Insurance Regulatory and Development Authority of India. BLIC is third on the list. Most of these fines are for failing to curtail fraudulent activities conducted by distributors.

'This sort of thing is no big deal, actually,' I say. 'I would say fines as small as these aren't even newsworthy.'

'It's not about the fine amount,' she says. 'It's about the offence being proven. I would say it is newsworthy.'

'OK, yeah, I get you,' I say. 'This one here… it's my company, in fact.'

'Ah, all right,' Jyoti says. 'Quite high on the list, I see. Is it a shady company?'

'I don't think so. Some of these mishaps, frauds – whatever you call them – they aren't even preventable. I think the regulator knows that too, which is why the fine amounts are small. I don't know much about the BLIC specific case here, but such things happen often because of oversight rather than any malicious intent.'

'So what kind of oversight slash malicious intent do you look after at BLIC?' Jyoti says.

'Has the tea done something to you?' I ask with a smile.

'No, nothing,' Jyoti says. 'I'm just interested in what you do at your company.'

'I am part of a team that looks after some of the more ambitious technology projects. Projects focussing on automation, digitalization – things leading to business transformation. Does that help?'

'Only if you tell me what business transformation means?' Jyoti says.

'Oh… let's say… let's just say that the old ways of running a life insurance company are a bit too elaborate and a bit too costly. Especially given what technology can do today.'

'So you're the guy who replaces these too-elaborate and too-costly ways with – what? – too-simple and too-cheap ways?' Jyoti counters. I find her tone to be a tad cynical, something that I realize might be part of her personality.

'You could say that. Though I'm not the only guy. There is a whole team, as I told you.'

'It's funny how you corporate-types always find it tough to explain what you do.'

'Ha.'

'I guess you don't like *elaborate* ways. But frankly I'd like you to *elaborate* a bit here.'

'Okay… so… yeah… let me try. So… do you know that it is possible to extract text from a scanned image?'

'Yes. Has been for some time, right?'

'Yeah, optical character recognition. OCR. But there was always a loss of information with OCR, always some text that could not be read, or was read wrong.'

'And now?'

'And now there is OCR enhanced with machine learning. If the context of the scanned document is known one can teach a machine to anticipate the lost text, which basically increases the accuracy of the whole text-reading thing to a level far better than previously known.'

'So you teach machines at BLIC to read text better?'

'Umm… I improve business processes using such technology.'

'Quite illuminating,' Jyoti says sarcastically.

'OK, well, let me give an example,' I say, not without some joy. 'Imagine yourself buying a new mobile connection. You'll probably have to fill out an application form where you'll need to write your address by hand, or you'll have to type it out into a digital form. You'll also have to provide proof of address, either a photocopy or a scan. In the phone company's back office, someone will need to ensure that the address that you've written on the form matches exactly – or indisputably – with what is provided on the proof of address. Now, if the telecom company was using the tech I mentioned, they would not need to make you write anything, or even to ask you for a photocopy. Their app would just scan the image of the address proof you offer – say, your passport – and it would then extract your address in a digital format. No paper, no human checking, no errors, no hassle.'

'O-kay,' Jyoti says. 'So you're the guy who conceives this whole thing?'

'Yes, in a way.'

'Interesting. But, you know, in reality, the phone company guys don't really ask you to write anything. They themselves write the address down from the proof you've given them... all you have to do is sign the form.'

'Well, I was just giving an example. These days with Aadhar KYC, the phone company guys just take your fingerprint and get your data from the government.'

'Ah... I hate that Aadhar thing. I'm never going to get one.'

'Really! You don't have an Aadhar? I don't think there is an escape from it.'

'It's scary – a scenario in which the government knows everything about their citizens. When have we ever had trustworthy governments?'

'I don't know about that,' I say.

'About what? The dangers of Aadhar?'

'Are there any real dangers? I don't think so.'

'You don't think there are any dangers or you have never given any thought to the dangers?' Jyoti asks.

'Yeah, whatever,' I shrug. 'So, what do you want for breakfast?'

'I have a question. What happens to the back-office guys?' asks Jyoti.

'Who?'

'The back-office guys in the telecom company… whose job it was to check whether my handwritten address matched with the one on my supporting document. What happens to them after the machine has learned to read?

'Obviously, no one is required to do those checks then,' I say.

'So you're saying those people will be fired?'

'Does that bother you?' I ask.

'Bother me? For sure it does,' says Jyoti. 'People getting fired should bother everyone, no? Tch… you guys are so besotted with the benefits of technology. Besotted to an extent that you fail to see what is really happening.'

'Come on, that's too simplistic. You don't understand – '

'No, I understand.'

'See, but, if one company employs superior tech, the others in their field… even if they don't want to… they will have to catch up. Their customers will push them to.'

'What happens to the people whose livelihoods are lost?' Jyoti asks, her voice now carrying a fair bit of agitation.

I am reminded of how, several months ago, a senior Ops person had commended the iSmart project in humanitarian terms. He had detailed how paper-handling outlets often employed minimum-wage people who did only one job: de-staple sheaves of paper. These de-staplers used their fingers to do their work; sometimes, they bled. 'Smudges used to appear in the document scans every now and then, sir. iSmart has put an end to this inhuman thing.' I recall the man's words. I had wondered then if the de-staplers losing their jobs was really the more humane outcome.

I don't narrate this out loud to Jyoti for the simple reason that it would weaken my argument. 'People find other employment,' I say instead, 'they reskill themselves.' This is spoken in an airy way that I don't much like myself, but in this conversation I find it mighty important to feign a particular kind of objectivity. The kind that operates at a high, abstract level. The kind that may not be very objective after all. Though why is it that I feel compelled to defend this turf is unclear to me. Am I being accused?

'You sound like a textbook,' Jyoti says, 'or like someone who writes a column in the NYT. If a child sleeps hungry for one night because some new technology made her father lose his job, for me that's a shame and that's on the corporation and on the people of the corporation.'

Jyoti's argument is too melodramatic, I think. But I also realize it is not easy to counter. The only way is to present the normal course of events as inevitable – that the world is what it is, that the world will become what it will become, that there is nothing to choose from, really. But I don't present this or any other argument. 'I think I will get on with the breakfast,' I say and move towards the kitchen.

'Really?' Jyoti hollers from behind me. 'You will get on with the breakfast?'

'Yes.'

'OK, then.'

'Scrambled? Omelette? Sunny side up?'

'The loo, I will go to the loo first.'

'Tell me what you want?'

'Whatever,' she shouts. I hear the toilet door shut.

I open the kitchen window, then take the butter and eggs out from the fridge. There is only a drizzle outside, though the sky is a deep gray. I feel disoriented, and I have a feeling that it is because of the conversation with Jyoti (it could be because of all the sex, too). While I'm beating the eggs, I think of the ways of the world. There is no progress that doesn't leave some people behind, no good that comes without a garnishing of bad – now that's a nice line. I put a pan on the flame and place a small chunk of butter in it. While hearing the sizzle, I tell myself that the best way to be is, perhaps, to lower one's head and carry on. To focus on making scrambled eggs well.

But what of the atrocities? the contrarian in me asks. Isn't this also the world where a child drowns while escaping a war?

Jyoti comes out of the toilet. The eggs are ready. The contrarian in me has left me unsettled, and I feel this desperate urge to say something harsh and true to her – to essentially unsettle her as much as I am. 'My current project,' I begin, loud so that she can hear me in the living room, 'is to use the latest machine learning technology to make five fifty plus people in my company redundant.'

She says nothing in response, nothing at all during the few minutes it takes me to prepare the plates and carry them to the small dining table in the living room. She joins me there with a stiff expression on her face.

'It'll do *what* to the people – your project?' she asks.

'Make them redundant,' I say.

'You are almost bragging here.'

'Am I? I don't think so – it's just the job.'

'You used "make redundant". Twice.'

There is anger in Jyoti's voice, and I immediately begin to regret having needed to do what I did. 'OK… well… I'm sorry, let's just have breakfast,' I say, sounding stupid even to myself.

She inhales, exhales, takes a couple of bites. I wonder if she's assessing whether everything since last night has been a mistake. The silence makes me panic. I put my hand on hers. She yanks it back.

'Hey,' she says, almost yelling, 'we are not there yet. OK?'

'What?'

'We are not there yet,' she repeats. Her eyes are wide with indignation. 'We don't have enough intimacy between us for you to keep your hand on mine.'

That makes me angry. 'But enough intimacy for you to sleep with me?' I ask. 'Enough intimacy to have breakfast together? Enough intimacy for you to be wearing my T-shirt while having it?'

In the span of a blink Jyoti gets up from the chair and removes the shirt. She balls it up and throws it down on her plate. Even her breasts shake with anger. She leans forward, her eyes boring into mine. 'So you're the guy who *feels* for that dead child,' she says. Then she goes inside the bedroom, where her clothes are, and begins to dress herself. I remove pieces of scrambled egg from the T-shirt.

'Why are you so angry?' I ask when she reappears in the living room, all set to leave.

She says nothing.

I find nothing to say.

'Fuck, I'm so stupid,' she mutters to herself, 'keep doing this shit, keep bumping into shitty men like you.'

'I do what I do, Jyoti,' I say in protest. 'I cannot change my job.'

'Dude, I'm not asking you to. I cannot be asking you to.'

'Maybe I used a word or two that I shouldn't have. But your reaction is way too extreme.'

'Look, Saransh, just tell yourself that I have a short temper. Which I do. I do have a short temper. So you aren't really wrong if you feel that. OK?'

'And?'

'And I'm leaving. It was great fucking you and all, and I wish you no success in your grand redundancy-inducing project. You can keep the Scrabble. You clearly need the practice.'

I stare at her blankly, which is all that I can do. She purses her lips, nods, and then steps out of the apartment with my umbrella, mistaking it for her own.

ZEPELLIN

NINE-THIRTY A.M. ON MONDAY MORNING. THE WORKWEEK IS clearing its throat. I live about two kilometers from work, so all I suffer in the name of a commute is a ten-minute auto ride. But there is a small glitch today. I have only twenty-eight rupees in my wallet – five short of what is needed to take me to the second gate of Bansal Tower, the building that houses the BLIC head office on its sixth floor. That's where I work, of course, as Deputy Vice President, Strategic Projects Group (SPG). Now, there is no ATM on the route, and since I work in a secluded team, chances of finding an acquaintance who can lend me a few rupees aren't high enough to be reliable. Being short by five rupees means that unless I find an unusually generous autowaala, my ride will have to end when I am a fair distance away from my intended destination. I will have to walk the last bit.

Bansal Tower is the first building inside the Great Hills IT Park, which, as the name suggests, is a business complex located inside what can be called an offshoot of the Western Ghats in Goregaon East. What this means is that I will have to walk the distance climbing up, something I don't really look forward to. Anyway, I catch an auto. After ten minutes, as the office building comes into view and the meter hits 28, I request the autowaala to stop. This puzzles the bulky man, who looks very much in the process of still waking up. I get off and pay all I have – the last coin included – and start walking towards Bansal Tower.

There is a throng of people around me, walking in the same direction as I am. Bansal Tower alone packs about five thousand people in it, and there are four other such towers in the IT Park. From the Goregaon train station, shared autos carrying three people each do rounds for this location all through the morning. The autowaalas, reluctant to drive up the slope, drop their passengers off at precisely the point where my auto has dropped me off today. So anyone working inside Great Hills and commuting by train always has to make the ascent to their respective tower – a steep walk of more than a hundred metres if the person doesn't work in Bansal Towers but in any of the other buildings.

I walk on looking down at the dog-biscuit-shaped bricks of the pavement. My back is stooping slightly and my fingers hold the straps of the work bag lugged on it. I'm surrounded by scores of men and women; some of them will soon become my colleagues or cohabitants or competitors for a good eight to ten hours. Looking at the others around me, the communal nature of what I'm doing becomes apparent. A flash of insight follows, in which I understand walking to office as sharing some essential element with the act of pilgrimage – a large group of people walking in a single direction, in a similar posture, all with bags on their backs; all of them mentally *inside* the place that they are approaching, all of them thinking of what they are to do there today, just as pilgrims always know what they are making the pilgrimage for. The honking of vehicles on the road is like chants egging us on. That the tall office buildings are located at a higher ground, that their glass bodies radiate a purposefulness, that they fulfill the requirement of looking as different from everyone's home (and their idea of home) as it is possible to be – all of this adds to what can be called a religious effect. Make an offer of your faith and austerity, and you will be provided sustenance in return – that's what these temples, like all temples, seem to tell us.

It takes only five minutes – the walk. I reach the second gate of Bansal Tower and scan my BLIC ID card and walk into the building. Now I've to find space inside a lift. Fortunately, an empty one arrives and I step into it along with at least ten other people. Everyone stands facing the lift door. Some study the overhead display showing the floor numbers we are moving past; others peer into their phones. 'What did you do during the weekend?' someone asks someone. 'Nothing much,' comes the answer.

Déjà vu of a déjà vu.

On our sixth-floor office they have made an attempt to name meeting rooms after flying objects. *Helicopter*, *Boeing*, *Jet*, *Glider*, et cetera. One of the larger meeting rooms is labelled *Zepellin*, subtracting a ‘p’ from and adding an ‘l’, to the spelling of the extinct German airship. I guess I’m the only one to have ever noticed the spelling error. People find it only mildly amusing when I point it out to them.

Anyhow, the Zepellin is now an exception. It has become, thanks to oversight, the only meeting room having nothing to do with aviation. A neologism, then, ready to receive any meaning. Which is an ambiguous sign, I feel, as it is the room that serves as our project den – the place where the Special Projects Group operates from. Think of it as the place for a team huddle. Only that this huddle is kind of perpetual.

As I enter the room I utter in my mind the two versions for the nth time, Zeppelin and Zepellin, exaggerating the possible difference in their pronunciations, enjoying both the lilt of the fake one and the pep of the original. Mitesh and George are already here, peering into their laptop screens with spectacular amounts of focus. ‘I don’t know how my weekend was,’ I say even before they can ask. Mitesh smiles; George offers no response at all. Just then Ankita enters. She’s on the phone saying, ‘Yeah, right? The photos have come out soooo nice. The baby looks soooo cute.’ Poonam should be coming in in a bit. The other two – Rizwan and Sayantan – are on a branch visit to Guwahati.

Zepellin has a large rectangular table at its centre with eight chairs around it – seven for the members and one reserved for Unnikrishnan, the SPG head, for the occasions when he visits us. The furniture takes up a good amount of the floor space. The upper halves of the long walls are made of glass which is frosted, in keeping with the aerodynamic theme, in a pattern that shows paper planes flying in loopy dotted lines. The pattern is hidden completely on one of the long walls because we have pasted charts and other colourful things on it. On one of the adjoining short walls hangs a large TV used for projecting stuff. Next to the TV is a narrow chest of drawers. On the opposing wall hangs an oil-on-canvas painting in a thick brown frame. White hills, rendered in long brushstrokes, constitute its background; the foreground is a brown hut standing beside shoots of deliberately disproportioned – as if the painter thought of it as the *subject* – bamboo grass. Today again I wonder if there could be anything stranger than this painting inside this room. Its presence is not loud, though. If I picked it up one evening and took it home, nobody would miss it the next day.

I affix my laptop to one of the charging points and settle in the chair between Mitesh and George. I enter two sets of usernames and passwords (the first to enter the computer, the second to enter the network) and mark my attendance. Then I stifle an inopportune yawn and in doing so happen to regard the long wall in front of me. It is an impressive display of our labours, bedecked with enlarged versions of complex flowcharts. The plethora of shapes – rectangles, rhombuses and ellipses, linked with a network of dotted or solid lines – can unsettle a newcomer with their burst of sophistication. Each flowchart is further adorned, along its sides and at the bottom, with a dozen or so Post-it notes which stick on, given the immaculately air-conditioned environment of the room, with a rather useful obstinacy, conveying a colourful, jargon-loaded sense of seriousness and urgency. One look at the wall must be enough to convince anyone that the occupants of this room are charged with a 'mission' mentality. We have indeed become a sort of secret society pursuing a holy grail that is, in shareholders' fantasies, quite simply the asymptote where an astronomical amount of insurance is sold at near-zero cost. That we are frequently ironic about the tasks before us, that we joke about the ignorant powers in the company, that we sometimes pronounce BLIC as *bleak*, that, mired in the details, we at times ridicule the possibility of achieving anything grand should not fool anybody. These are coping mechanisms, and coping mechanisms only prove that there is something to cope with. Some of us have been in Zepellin for almost three years, and so it is not surprising when there is the occasional pining for the modest privacy of a cubicle. But no one would seriously suggest it. Least of all me, for it is I who made this Zepellin congregation happen in the first place. Or at least that's what the others like to tease me about.

The story of how we came into Zepellin might as well start in late 2013 when the latest entrant in the Indian life insurance industry announced itself as a *digital-first* player, vowing to spend more on technology than on the setting up of a traditional brick-and-mortar distribution model. Two of the largest incumbents also started talking of technology as a differentiator, as means to a lasting competitive advantage. The external environment couldn't have been offering clearer signals. A boom had taken place in Indian e-commerce – Flipkart, Snapdeal, Myntra and many others like them were being talked of as blazing success stories. A digital economy had more or less established itself in India's top ten cities. Ranked #7 among the twenty-one private life insurance providers in the country, BLIC was middling enough to feel the fear of missing out and big enough to sniff an opportunity. To their credit, our top brass didn't dress up a high-flyer from outside as a sacrificial goat before the shareholders. Instead they chose the sharpest old horse amongst them, a man named Adarsh Unnikrishnan, as Head of Digitalization. In his late forties then, Unnikrishnan had held key positions in several Bansal group companies and thus commanded considerable respect in BLIC. He was said to be a master at *making change happen*. Once in charge, he set out to understand our internal landscape – the technologies we had started out with, the changes in people and technology over time, the compromises we had learned to live with, et cetera. After four months of that, he announced – at a meeting in early 2014 that is now regarded *landmark* in BLIC – that only a handpicked team unencumbered by the usual inter-departmental conflicts would be able to do anything substantial. He also used a phrase nobody had heard until then: *innovation sandbox*. Naturally, he was given carte blanche for forming that sandbox.

Unnikrishnan knew that, first of all, he would need someone from the technology side to accept the challenge

– someone who knew how our legacy systems worked but who could also be made horny, so to speak, by the idea of change. Mitesh Shah, Vice President, was identified as the only person in the IT department as dynamic enough and ambitious enough and – this, too, is important – loyal enough for the role. Unnikrishnan plucked him out of IT and made him the first member of the sandbox.

I was less than two years old in the company at that point, and was working in a department called Business Process Excellence, where I was leading a team of three moderately motivated management trainees. You could have called me HO's everything and nothing man – the well-paid, big-B-school boy, kept as a sort of intellectual reserve for some big game-changing agenda. I ran simulations for Rewards & Recognition programs, tried to introduce standardization in paper-based sales processes, weeded out inefficiencies in Operations and HR, and so on. My projects focussed on incremental improvements, never *disruption*; and this was something that was beginning to frustrate me. Mitesh, with whom I had collaborated on a couple of low-key projects, knew about this frustration. In mid-April 2014, a few days after his own inclusion in the sandbox, he suggested my name to Unnikrishnan. Right on cue, Unnikrishnan sent me and my boss a memo. I was relieved of my Business Process Excellence duties and asked to join the sandbox asap.

The next to come in was Ankita, a high-performing Zonal Sales Head from Mumbai. Her claim to fame was using a free family-member-locating app for monitoring the precise movements of her sales representatives during the day. Her penchant for uttering vapid clichés aside, Ankita was a master at sales management. Later, she would help us make the best use of the geo-tagging feature on iSmart.

Ankita was followed by George Iype, the Zonal Operations Head from Chennai. George managed no less than sixty branch offices. He had been with BLIC since the beginning (2001) and had risen from the LOE level. He was regarded as the best in his role in the company, someone who could transform slipshod HO directives into a workable process overnight and then execute ten variations of the same process across different offices. But the call up to Mumbai was actually a godsend for him. There were two complaints of sexual harassment against him that were *in processing*. Besides, he had thrice been reported for watching porn in the Chennai branch office. Each time his defence had moved from denial to feigning accident to ultimately arguing that it wasn't the hardcore stuff but the softer variety. The Committee Against Sexual Harassment (CASH) was said to be centimetre-close to a *terminate* decision. But then things changed, as if at the click of a button. All the charges against George Iype vanished and his status changed from expendable to vital. What had happened was that Mitesh had recommended him to Unnikrishnan, and Unnikrishnan had used the CEO to nudge the CASH committee head, who had in turn found a way to browbeat or cajole or bribe those who had complained against George. George landed in Mumbai with his family as quickly as it was humanly possible. I am sure a stern warning regarding conduct towards female colleagues was delivered at some point, a sort of clarification that this was his last chance. The warning has worked – we haven't caught him watching anything remotely pornographic, and his behaviour towards Ankita or Poonam or any other woman at HO has betrayed no signs of past predilections in the last three years that he's been here. Ankita, in fact, travels with him routinely for our current project, though there are reasons why no mishap can occur there – Ankita has retained the brazenly outspoken persona required to be successful in sales, which is a safeguard in addition to the fifteen kilo advantage she has over George should it ever come to a scuffle or a tickle.

What I knew about George's scandals was common knowledge in the entire company at the time. Mitesh never consulted me before onboarding him. He spoke only with Unnikrishnan; he had direct, exclusive access to the boss then just as he does now. But would I have objected had he asked me? I can't be sure. I might have expressed discomfort, but I don't think I would have told Mitesh not to recommend George. It wasn't my place to do so.

These – Mitesh, Ankita, George and I – were the first members of the sandbox. We couldn't continue calling it the sandbox (for risk of being labelled ostriches, if nothing else), so we named it the Strategic Projects Group. The SPG reported to the Head of Digitalization, Adarsh Unnikrishnan. In June 2014, we held our first meeting in a room called *Mig*. 'You have complete freedom to define the digitalization agenda of this company,' Unnikrishnan said right at the beginning. We felt empowered, energized. But when, close to the end of the one-hour meeting, someone from the Claims department asked us to vacate the room because our scheduled time at Mig was up, we felt that we had no space of our own. The couple of days Unnikrishnan gave us to draft a charter was mostly spent in searching for meeting rooms to have discussions in. Consequently, I – brimming with the zeal of a neophyte – proposed that we abandon our cubicles and grab a meeting room permanently. 'Sitting together is the best way to collaborate' – as tacky as they may sound now, those were my words. Unnikrishnan heard them through Mitesh. And that is how Zepellin was sanctioned for our permanent use.

The charter we drafted pleased Unnikrishnan. We were going to be data-driven. We were going to use technology to bring about business transformation. We were going to keep pace with the fast-changing landscape. We were going to work on the biggest problem statements. We were going to aid top-level decision-making...

The first big thing we zeroed in on was replacing paper flows with data flows. Insurance application forms should be digitized at the point of sale itself, we recommended, so that paper forms are eliminated. When that happened, instead of paper travelling physically, electronic files would fly through secure systems invisibly and precisely. In other words, digital modes of form-filling, document capture and customer authentication (KYC) needed to be placed in the hands of all salespersons. This would be done through an app that worked on mobile phones and tablets. Ergo: iSmart.

After months of planning, design, development and testing, the first version of iSmart came out in September

2015. Feature after feature got added to the app for more than a year. By October 2016, we had nearly eliminated paper trails and other benefits were beginning to accrue. For instance, iSmart provided us with unprecedented behavioural data at the point of sale. For the first time ever, the black box of sales interaction – the long chat(s) between the insurance salesperson and the customer – became a white box for people sitting at the HO. The data was periodically shared with the training team, who after some analysis were able to figure out which salesperson lacked in which specific aspect of selling. Personalized learning modules were then distributed through iSmart. In the very first month of doing so a 3 per cent lift was seen in sales productivity on a year-on-year basis.

But the journey was not as smooth as I make it sound. In March 2016, the last month of the financial year, iSmart faced technical snags and broke down during peak hours for a couple of days. There was backlash from sales teams, including murmurs that the app was not well thought-through, that it had failed to take into account the ground realities. In response, Unnikrishnan introduced something called a monthly Steering Committee (SCOM), in which a wider representation from our senior management, including a couple of national sales heads, could review SPG's progress. 'Give a thorough account, but don't simplify anything for anyone,' these were Unnikrishnan's directions to the Zepellin squad. Only later did I realize why he did what he did – to increase the illusion of transparency, while retaining the same tight grip on our functioning. It worked amazingly well. While each senior SCOM member could deliver testimonies as to how the digital world was changing their lives, or remark about the strategies of big consumer-tech companies like Apple or Google, no one really had the know-how to question SPG jargon. In time, iSmart's back-end wrinkles were smoothed and the SCOM became a monthly exercise in corporate timepass. When in June 2016, a senior underwriter named Poonam joined the SPG, she was joining a proven team, practically beyond questioning and itching for a bigger game.

Two p.m. We are meeting representatives of a newly-minted Indian company named *Brahma.ai*. The meeting is taking place in the room called Helicopter (it could not have happened inside Zepellin; the charts and Post-its there are not for outsiders' viewing). Not everyone in the SPG wanted this meeting right now. Our hands are full for the rest of this financial year, and we may not be able to implement anything that Brahma presents today. But Mitesh plans ahead, and he's right. Meetings like this one are important for us to zero in on the projects we might want to pursue next year.

Brahma's founder, Raju, is a T-shirt-clad, desperately-needing-a-haircut-and-a-shave man of barely twenty-five years. He is a recent Computer Science graduate from IIT Bombay. The person accompanying him, Brahma's Head of Business Development, is the gray-haired, buttoned-down persona we are more used to seeing. His name is Sarath. Tough as it is to stomach, Raju is Sarath's boss. So it is Raju who opens their presentation. 'Let's be real,' he says, 'man-made algorithms suck. And they suck big time.'

We all titter.

'No, I'm serious,' Raju says. 'Man-made rules suck. Can you guys tell me why?'

'Because they are faulty?' Mitesh says.

'Yes, they are,' Raju says. 'Though, for me, even the ones we might call accurate suck. Can you guess why?'

'Because they are made by man?' Ankita says. When she is not talking in clichés, Ankita can usually be found stating the obvious.

'Yes. And what is the defining quality of anything done by man?'

'That it sucks,' George says, smiling and looking at others for approbation.

'I would put it differently,' Raju says. 'The defining quality of human activity is that it is driven by emotion, not reason.' He pauses to let everyone confirm the truth of the last sentence to themselves. He is a cocky bastard, this Raju.

'This,' he says, and points to the slide on view. There is only one word on it: EMOTION. 'This is the most important thing. And facts and reason have got nothing on it. Man-made algorithms suck, ladies and gentlemen, because they are based on emotion. Which is to say that they are products of personal experiences. Of biases. Of personality quirks. Of recency effects. Man-made algorithms are an all-too-human interpretation of the thing, not the thing in itself.'

Raju pauses again. I'm reminded of my short dalliance with Immanuel Kant during my third year of engineering. *Ding an sich*, the thing in itself.

Sarath begins phlegmatically: 'I find that there is something classic and time-tested in life insurance's basic premise, something about being practical in an emotional situation – if you pay us a premium every year, for a certain number of years, we will pay your loved one an assured sum in case you die anytime during those years. The operating principle at the heart of this is classic, too. We are able to assure that sum today because when taken in aggregate over large numbers, the observations of mortality in a healthy population, of which you're a part, is predictably distributed across ages. In other words, we sort of know how many of you will die in those years. Am I correct here?'

'Yes…' some of us, including me, respond. I don't think I've heard a better euphemism for deaths than *observations of mortality*. But that's how life insurance goes.

Sarath continues: 'Of course, everything works under the assumption that the person buying insurance is not hiding compromising information about his health or finances. That said, doing a thorough assessment of each and every application is impossible. That's why there are underwriting rules, rules that, on the basis of some predefined parameters, determine which customers should be given insurance and which ones should be denied.'

'And underwriting rules are man-made algorithms,' Raju jumps in. 'Based on personal experiences and biases. Based on emotion. This is what we are here to talk about today.'

From this point on, the Brahma guys turn quickly to their actual sales pitch. Over the course of a dozen or so progressively loaded slides, their presentation details how the historical data of an insurance company can teach a machine to take underwriting decisions on the fly, thereby obviating the need for man-made underwriting rules. It's a spectacular pitch, I concede in my head, despite the contradiction with Raju's spiel against emotions, the contradiction being implicit in the suggestion that a truckload of data generated by *emotional* algorithms made by *emotional* humans can somehow help create a machine better than humans.

It's not just about the rules and the emotions thereof, I remind myself. A big portion of our applications today are underwritten by people sitting in the HO, people who can make sense of all the financial and medical data that these applications are appended with. They are the ones who decide whether the risk of the applicant's life will be borne by the company or not. Implementing Brahma's underwriting solution means firing these people. Of course, Raju or Sarath don't have to spell this out.

When the presentation ends, Sarath asks us for the 'next steps'. Mitesh tells him that the team is busy implementing another project and would need at least a few weeks before going back to him 'post an internal discussion.' After the Brahma guys leave, the SPG stays back in the Helicopter.

'What do you think?' Mitesh asks everyone. He doesn't wait for an answer, though: 'I think this should be our next project. This seems easier than what we are doing with the LOEs. We should evaluate now and take this up immediately after the LOE project.'

'This sounds exciting,' says Ankita.

'How many underwriters are there in the company today?' George asks.

'About forty,' Poonam answers.

'Forty people is a lot of savings,' Mitesh says. 'And these are not low salary resources, not like the LOEs.'

'The entire underwriting desk will go, right?' George says.

'Half of the East Zone here,' I say, nodding towards the cubicles and seating bays outside the Helicopter.

'Can we include this proposal in the SCOM presentation, Saransh?' Mitesh asks me. 'We can have a preliminary discussion there. I will cover Unni beforehand.'

'This is big, Mitesh,' I tell him. 'Take a breath. These are people with specializations. Good salaries. Expertise.'

'So?' he asks.

'These are people in Head Office. People we see every day.'

'If it can be done, sooner or later it will be done.' Mitesh says.

'We don't even know if this can be done,' says Poonam.

Mitesh looks at her but says nothing. In the next couple of minutes we all leave Helicopter and move towards Zepellin. The shortest path goes through the East

Zone, where I cannot help but gaze at the area where the underwriting department sits. It shouldn't matter. If the impending expiration of 550+ LOEs doesn't matter, then the impending expiration of 40 underwriters shouldn't matter either.

Back in Zepellin, I open the presentation for the next SCOM and add a new slide about the Brahma proposal, putting in a series of bullet points the premise that emotion always creeps into whatever it is that humans do. While doing so, I think of all the emotion that goes into conceiving emotionless machines.

Around the time the biggest obstacles hit iSmart, the chain of events leading to our next big project was also set in motion. Inside a five-star hotel in Seoul, Lee Sedol, a grandmaster at the game of Go, was comprehensively beaten by Google Deepmind AI's AlphaGo program in a five-match series. In the second game, one particular move by AlphaGo was so unprecedented, so otherworldly, so para-human that Sedol had had to go and wash his face. Or so they say. After Sedol's loss Go experts reported feeling inconsolably sad – not for Sedol but for humanity.

The game turned out to be the PR equivalent of a lottery for two buzzwords that were already gaining momentum in the IT services industry – Artificial Intelligence (AI) and Machine Learning (ML). IT sellers began pitching offerings around these even more aggressively. What these words meant was never clarified; some sellers stressed the technical difference between the two, others used them interchangeably. The story of Lee Sedol's loss – and his bewilderment during the loss – was told and retold, leaving no doubt that the machines were here to play the most complex games we could think of, and to beat us. So-called thought leaders started hyping the advent of the final industrial revolution. The Indian ones among them took to terrorizing their audiences by pointing out how well China was preparing for the new technologies.

In August 2016, IBM deployed its AI product, Watson, in the Oncology department of a hospital chain in India. This was the first major implementation of the technology in the country. Soon after this news came out, Unnikrishnan came to Zepellin for a quick meeting. 'We need to understand the hype, understand the technology, and understand which problems of ours this thing is best suited for,' he said. He then looked at me with level eyes, pointed his finger, and said, 'Saransh, how about you focus on this for three weeks?'

This was the first time Unnikrishnan had given me a task directly. I put in extra hours to research. I studied a few modules on Coursera. Through LinkedIn, I connected with a couple of friends from my tech school, those who were now on the bleeding edge of ML, and had discussions with them. Three weeks later, I told Unnikrishnan and the group that while there existed dozens of areas where ML could be tried, what it could most certainly do at BLIC, to begin with, was automate all document-checking operations within the company. My slides also showed a list of business processes where document-checking was done at that time. 'So, it can eliminate the task of branch-level scrutiny?' Mitesh asked, picking one item from my list. 'Yes, I think so,' I said. This seemed to excite Mitesh, who then turned towards Unnikrishnan and exclaimed: 'That's done by LOEs today. There's more than 500 of them on our rolls.' Unnikrishnan didn't react and just kept on looking at the slides. Near the end of the meeting he said 'good work' to me. Then he announced that we had until November to get whatever resources we needed to pursue ML projects. A few days later, realizing that the quality of past data would determine the success of ML efforts, Mitesh and I recommended the hiring of a data scientist. Unnikrishnan green-lit it immediately, and by September we had Rizwan Ahmad, a statistician with years of analytics experience in the sports-betting industry in England, join the SPG.

Within the SPG, Ankita, George, Poonam and Sayantan (a software testing expert who joined around the same time as Rizwan) began to focus more on iSmart, while Mitesh, Rizwan and I assumed charge of the ML preparations. The latter involved meeting experts, trying to ascertain the computing power we would need on the cloud or on BLIC premises, learning about which approaches suited which problems, and so on. We invited demos from companies selling OCR technology combined with an ML engine. The idea was that as the machine learned the confidence level with which text was gleaned from images would become high. For us, this simply meant that the central activity involved in scrutiny – the reading of text from one source and matching it with text on another source – could be done automatically.

We were just about closing our ML game plan by early November when another historical thing happened – Demonetization. With one announcement, Prime Minister Narendra Modi made most of the cash available in the country worthless – until, of course, a bank could see it. The entire Bansal group, like every other financial powerhouse, had to put all its energies into managing (and making most of) the situation. Focus only returned to the ML project after the Demo dust had settled. And so, it was in January this year when the strategy was finally pitched to the SCOM. The plan was pretty much what I had earlier proposed in a meeting inside Zepellin, but in the SCOM, Unnikrishnan had wanted Mitesh to present the case. Mitesh's pitch consisted of five points *(1) We will capitalize on iSmart. (2) We will use ML to read the incoming digital documents. (3) We will also use ML to decide whether a proposal should pass scrutiny or not. (4) We will automate the work that the LOEs do today. (5) We will fire the LOEs.* Mitesh also proposed a name for the project: *iBlink*. The SCOM members quickly calculated that removing 550-odd LOEs off the payroll would save about ₹15 crores per annum in wage bill and also release valuable seating space in the branches (whose value was estimated to be another ₹10 crores). The project's cost, even if one were to include hefty bonuses to all members of the SPG, would not exceed ₹4 crores, one-time. It was a no-brainer.

Things went smoothly for a few months until we did our first tests on live data. The results made Rizwan shake his head again and again. 'The base data isn't right, it seems,' he said. *How do we make it right?* 'I don't even know which records are wrong.' *So what do you know?* 'We will need to talk to the LOEs. Extensively.' *Are you joking?* 'No, look, what I'm saying is we do not have enough information to make this work from HO. We need help from the LOEs. *So you're suggesting we ask them to help us – to get them fired?* 'Yes… No… you guys need to understand what I'm trying to say.'

We did come to understand what Rizwan was saying. The results were unsatisfactory because of the lack of standardization in how LOEs handled on-the-ground situations. The machine always gave a probabilistic output. But there was no way to say whether its output was correct or incorrect because in the historical data the same input had produced all kinds of decisions from different LOEs. In other words, there were too many scenarios that we, the SPG people, did not know of, and which, therefore, the machine didn't know of either. This meant that past data could not be considered rich enough or true enough. And a machine cannot learn the truth from untruth.

This only meant one thing – we would have to start again. Unnikrishnan made a stoical face when we told him and left us with only three words, each one of which felt like a paragraph – 'Make. It. Work.' We knew we needed to identify the scenarios that were impacting the machine's output in ways we didn't understand. But how would we find the bad datum, the anomaly, without any identifying feature? The chart that I had prepared with the formal definition, and pasted on one of Zepellin's high walls, gave only a broad direction.

> *This is a search for anomalies. An anomaly is any scenario in which*
>
> *(1) there exists a high degree of variance in human decision-making or processing practices and,*
>
> *(2) more importantly, no one at HO knows what the right decision or practice is.*

It took us some time to acknowledge that no sharper method (other than Rizwan's original gut feel) was available, and that discovering anomalies would require some good old *learning*, that of the decidedly human kind, the kind that happens through conversations. We would have to talk extensively with the LOEs. There was no way we could hire anyone to do this on our behalf, which meant that the SPG, members of which hardly ever came out of the Zepellin, would now have to travel around the country and meet LOEs. Brute force, that's what this method really was. Brute force and prayer. It made me wonder if we had rushed into the LOE project too soon. But now there was no going back. In fact, another set of issues now needed solving: under what pretence would we converse with the LOEs? What, precisely, would we ask them? How would we withhold information while extracting it?

It is when the group was faced with these questions that George was pulled from iSmart into iBlink. After all, it was he and others like him who had, over a period of time, introduced the very same anomalies that we had to catch now. Putting into use all his experience as a LOE and as someone who used to manage LOEs on a daily basis, George drafted a how-to manual for the group.

The LIFE guide, or the SPG handbook for conducting a heist in four distinct acts, is a masterpiece of manipulation. Firstly, it provides a slew of rapport-building manoeuvres – aimed at discovering the LOE's family background, the jobs they held before this one, their daily troubles with the commute, et cetera. The idea is to evince interest not only in their professional lives but in their lives in general, so that they lower their guard and feel that they can speak freely. The guide then provides tactics to ascertain how the LOE brings in their own personality, their own unique stamp, their own touch to their daily work. For example: 'Can you narrate an instance when you did something unique, something that you feel particularly proud of?' At this point, the focus is on eliciting concrete examples, which the guide requires to be noted down and always appreciated. Then the guide recommends that the LOE in question be asked to suggest improvements, to respond to questions like 'What can we do to help you do your work even better?', or, 'Are there any niggles in your work that you'd like to be solved through technology?' This is to make the LOE feel that he or she is contributing to the company's cause, although for us it is just another way to ask the earlier question. Finally, the guide provides closing techniques, almost all of which encourage the SPG interviewer to share some or other irrelevant HO information with the LOE – the bad food in the canteen, the habits of the CEO, how things move very slowly at HO, and so on – so that the LOE leaves the room feeling equal, feeling as if he or she has learned valuable information about the company.

And that is how, armed with our LIFE guides, we started going out in search of anomalies with the intention to visit as many branches and meet as many LOEs that we could.

I plod on with the slides for the SCOM presentation. The new anomalies we discovered, our LOE coverage till now, the date on which the machine will start learning again.

I'm a bit bored. While reading the text inside a blue box on a slide, my mind goes back to Sunday morning and I recall Jyoti and her breakfast-time spurt of hostility. George is next to me, talking to Rizwan on the phone. I wonder what Jyoti would think of me if she came to know that I work with a man like George, even sit next to him every day. That my success and his success go hand-in-hand. That if the easing of 550-odd employees from the system is a vile conspiracy (something that Jyoti surely believes), then sexual predator George Iype and I, her recent sexual partner, are in cahoots.

I realize that even a different version of George, in which he's not a pervert, might be a problem for Jyoti. A *turncoat*, she might say. George is, after all, one of those who defined and embedded the LOE role in the day-to-day functioning of the company. *And look at him now, working with a remote team to banish the people working in that same role.*

And what would Jyoti say of our method of discovering anomalies, of questioning the LOEs with a notebook open on one side and the LIFE guide on the other? She will probably see the initial part of the interaction, the part where we establish rapport, as the most sinister. *Cold-hearted butchers making a show of being kind to the lamb,* I hear her voice in my head.

But I am not cold-hearted, am I? All the faux interest in the lives of LOEs did at times become a real thing for me. Once, in an interview that Mitesh and I did in Mumbai, a LOE named Sanjiv started crying. The building in which he lived with his parents had collapsed during the previous year's monsoon and his parents had been crushed under the rubble. Sanjiv had survived only because he was at the office, working overnight during the month-end. I hugged him after the interview and brought him some tea from the pantry. In Pune, a LOE named Tanima told us about being slapped by a male colleague she refused to name. It had happened inside the branch, in broad daylight, in front of everyone. Back in HO, I reported the incident to the HR folks. When nothing happened, I even followed up with them a couple of times. I didn't escalate the matter only because Mitesh asked me to take it easy. 'If people at other branches get to know about your complaint, they might not cooperate with us,' he reasoned.

And you stopped? I hear Jyoti say inside my head again.

I exhale through my mouth, rub my eyes, shut the

laptop. I consider the phenomenon of Jyoti speaking inside my head. Of course, it is not Jyoti but my estimation of Jyoti. But does this – the approximation of another's voice, even their thoughts, inside one's head – mean something? I wonder what has altered, for the thoughts that I'm ascribing to Jyoti have never before come to me inside Zepellin. Or anywhere else.

I stand up and ask aloud if anyone wants to join me for a cup of coffee. Mitesh agrees.

We leave Zepellin and walk towards the break-out area. Since I am flustered by the estimative Jyoti in my head, I decide to relieve myself by telling Mitesh about the real Jyoti.

'I met a girl,' I say. We are sitting on the funky chairs in the break-out area, adding sugar to our machine-made cappuccinos. Before he can respond, a woman from housekeeping comes and sprays the square table top between us with a light-blue liquid and wipes it clean. I consider if I should have said woman instead of girl when talking about Jyoti, and decide against correcting myself. I have said what I've said matter-of-factly, as if yes of course what else could have happened over the weekend, what else could I be discussing next to the coffee machine. Mitesh shifts in his chair. He is wearing a white shirt and a slant-striped tie, the colour of alternate stripes approaching that of his dark-brown trousers. He has the company cufflinks on too. Mine are probably floating in the Bay of Bengal by now. I note how Mitesh is always like this – immaculate. I never wear a tie when I'm in HO. Or cufflinks. Only one level separates us in the organization's pecking order, but Mitesh is far superior in managing optics, in elevating himself through a carefully cultivated aura of professionalism.

'This weekend?' he finally asks, after thoroughly stirring the sugar in his coffee and taking a sip. 'You met a girl this weekend?'

'Yes.'

'What about?'

'What about?'

He laughs. 'How was she? Did you like her?'

'You could say that, yes.'

'That means you did the thing?'

'You're asking me about sex?'

'Yes.'

'Well, yes,' I smile.

He smiles back and gives me a thumbs up. 'So what's her name? What does she do?'

'Jyoti,' I say. It occurs to me that Jyoti is a bit of an old-fashioned name these days. But so is Mitesh. And Saransh.

Mitesh doesn't react to the name, just buries his nose in the coffee cup.

'She's an ex-journalist of some sort,' I add.

'Interesting,' he says, furrowing his brows, as if somewhat concerned for me.

'You'll think of it as funny but… we actually had a fight yesterday morning,' I say. There is no reason for me to share this with Mitesh. But I felt his 'interesting' needed to be responded to with something really interesting.

'Oh really! So you met a girl, had sex, and then had a fight.' Mitesh touches his tie twice as he says this, once at the knot and once at the end. This means that he is interested. 'That's a good template,' he adds, chuckling.

'Our fight was about work,' I say.

'What work? Her journalism?' he asks. 'Is she a Modi-hating journo? Or are *you* a Modi-hater?'

'No, no. It was about my work. About our project. What we are going to do.'

'What are we going to do?' Mitesh leans in.

'I mean… I told her that we are trying to design an automated system… a system that will do the work that requires a considerable number of people today.'

'You told her that we are going to fire a lot of people?'

'Umm… in a way, yes.'

'And?'

'And she didn't like that. I mean, she walked out on me after hearing that. That's something, right?'

'Hmm,' Mitesh looks a bit concerned. 'She might be a commie journalist.'

'What?'

'A communist. There are many of that type, too. She might report this, you chutiya. Let me see. What's her full name?' He takes out his cellphone.

'I don't know. And no, she won't. She's not a journalist anymore, I told you. She left the profession because of some ethical concerns. She seemed to be an ethical person. You know what I mean, right?'

'So are we,' Mitesh says. 'But that doesn't mean anything. Is this her?'

He shows me a profile on Twitter. It is her. With the same profile photo as on Tinder. With the same profile description as on Tinder (except the 'ex-journalist' bit, the ex is not there on Twitter). For a moment, I wonder what it means for a person to have (nearly) identical profiles on these two very different platforms. That she knows that it is her convictions that make her attractive? That her erotic persona is the same as her political persona? I notice she has 3,000+ followers on Twitter. I have thirty.

'Yes, that's her,' I tell Mitesh. 'How did you find her?

'I just searched for Jyoti and journalist together,' he says. Then he gestures to ask: what were you thinking?

The possibility that I've jeopardized the company's plans by revealing them to Jyoti is not how I thought of it until now. There is no expressly-stated company policy regarding this. But the general code of conduct bars employees from *fostering speculation in the external environment*. 'There is no risk from her,' I tell Mitesh as well as myself. 'That's not why I told you about her.'

'Then?'

'No specific reason, man. Or I guess I just wanted to share this with you. To let you know that certain people can't agree with what we are doing… what we are doing and what it will result in.'

'I know that, Saransh,' Mitesh says. 'But these are people,' he points to his cellphone screen, 'who find ways to criticize everything. All you get from them is negativity.'

'Don't generalize.'

Mitesh ignores my comment. 'What we are doing, what our job is – someone else will do it if we don't,' he says. 'And what has to happen will happen, no? At the end of the day it's about making progress, man.'

'I told her something similar. You know what she said? She said that there was nothing called progress. That progress was a fiction.'

Mitesh makes a mocking sound and then we both smile and shake our heads and empty our coffee mugs. Jyoti never said anything about progress. Why did I make that up?

'She also said this other thing just before leaving. Something like, if a child sleeps hungry because the father lost his job to new technology then it is the fault of the people who brought in that technology.'

'That's just dumb,' Mitesh says.

'I guess it boils down to saying why do something that could make a child hungry?'

'Yeah, yeah, why adopt technology, why have systems, why have improvement… why not sit at home and feed our children. Wonder how that will happen, though.'

For a brief moment I consider telling him about Alan Kurdi. About how he's connected to my interaction with Jyoti. Or perhaps in a different way; about how, when in September 2015 we were busy launching the first version of iSmart, a dead child, escaping war in his own country, was found on the coast of Turkey. But Mitesh will think of it as a non sequitur, and he will be right to do so.

We finish our coffee and move out of the break-out area and walk towards Zepellin. I think of the one game – the fourth in the five-match series – in which Lee Sedol beat AlphaGo. Somebody should talk about the beauty of that.

GIVEN EICHMANN IS GUILTY

TUESDAY, 12TH SEPTEMBER. AFTERNOON. I'M AT THE DELHI airport, having arrived there from Bathinda to catch a flight back to Mumbai.

me: So are you really not going to talk?
Because I have the job I have?
Because that makes me a horrible person?

Jyoti reads the three lines immediately after I send them. Nothing happens for the next ten minutes and the lines become loaded with my shame – my shame of being the one to reach out – as I stare at them. Then I see Jyoti typing. Then she's not typing. Then she's typing again.

Jyoti: I talk.
me: ?
Jyoti: I do talk… I've not stopped talking.
me: Unfunny… in case you thought that was funny.
I mean talk to me, of course.

She doesn't say anything to that and after waiting for three minutes I begin to feel angry.

me: You picked a fight and you walked out. Was it just convenience?
I mean… if it had gone as far as you wanted it to…
You didn't have to be rude…

No answer again for two minutes. Now I begin to regret what I've said.

Jyoti: I'm sorry
me: !
Jyoti: I reacted too strongly.
But I'm like this. I react strongly. Feel strongly.
Tell me one thing…
me: What?
Jyoti: Are you a Modi supporter?
me: Why's that important?
Jyoti: Sometimes I think it is the only important thing.
me: And I presume if I say I am his supporter you will stop chatting with me?
Jyoti: Are you? (and is *presume* really a word you use often?)
me: I'm not. I don't care about politics…
I'm the person to whom it doesn't matter who the president or the PM is.
(yes, I do use it)
Jyoti: Well…

Not being interested in politics is deeply political.

me: OK… so I guess I'm political. By not being into politics.

Jyoti: Yes… very much so.

me: But is that better than being a Modi supporter?

Jyoti: Only slightly better.

me: Now let me ask you something.

Jyoti: Okay.

me: Are you a communist of some sort?

Jyoti: Ahahahaha

me: That's a serious question, yaar. You quit journalism because of the corporatization and shit, didn't you?

Jyoti: No I'm not a communist.

Though I could become one.

I guess I could.

Not of the Stalin variety though.

So don't worry… you are not going to the gulag :P

me: So… bcs I work in a company and you're a potential communist you'd always hate me?

Jyoti: I don't hate you.

me: But you could?

Jyoti: Our fight that morning was not because I'm a communist and you're a corporate dude or whatever… hope that's clear to you.

You are working on a project that will make hundreds lose employment.

It's your job job, yes.

But at a personal level, that sort of thing should do something to you.

And it doesn't.
The way you talked about it...

Jyoti stops typing. Her final ellipses are supposed to remind me of the way I talked about it. Did I really talk about it?

me: The way I talked about it?
Jyoti: Yes!
It was as if you weren't bothered. Worse, in fact... it was as if you were incapable of... of even trying to know why it is a wrong thing.
me: Incapable??
THANKS for this glowing assessment of my intellect.
Jyoti: I didn't mean it that way.
And incapable is perhaps the wrong word. Unwilling, more like.
You are too in it, you know.
me: But I see it as a tragic thing too... I do.
Jyoti: A tragedy that is beyond your influence?
me: Is it not? If I don't participate in it, do you think it'll not happen?
Jyoti: Its inevitability cannot be your excuse for participating in it.
That's like a murderer saying that the victim was anyway going to die one day.
me: Eh?
Jyoti: Eichmann could have said the same thing.
me: Eichmann?
Jyoti: Yes... Eichmann.

me: And that's not taking it too far?

Jyoti: I guess it is. (you know about Eichmann!)

me: It's the sort of thing companies do… always have done.
(hope my being aware of Eichmann means that your assessment of my intellect has suddenly and dramatically improved!)

Jyoti: And they must be detested for this.
(so you've read Narendr)
(Oh I meant Arendt (wow… autocorrect is scary!))

me: For what exactly?
(yup… I have the book (in an alternate universe that autocorrect fail just caused a war))

Jyoti: For containing… cultivating… the idea of a money making machine in which the person or the individual or whatever you call a fucking human being is incidental…
Or *redundant*
(and all you were displaying on your bookshelf were business books, you dumbass!)

me: Phew! It is called Capitalism for a reason. Not labour is or people is. And I am not the one who came up with the idea.
Labourism or Peopleism
(I also have Mein Kampf btw :D … bought it as a teenager from a stall at Kashmiri Gate bus stand in Delhi.)

Jyoti: And doesn't it bother you that one day your Capitalism won't need people?
(you sure you don't support Modi?)

me: *My* Capitalism!?

The Matrix isn't here yet… and if it is then I'm not Neo… that's all I know.

(actually… even if I supported him, I would be willing to reconsider my allegiance… if only I could have you explain these complex things to me)

Jyoti: Eww, dude. You just hit on me. From inside a parentheses.

me: Did I?

Jyoti: Yes of course you did.

me: Btw…

You are the third person I know who doesn't say hahahaha but ahahahaha

Jyoti: You obviously want me to ask you who the first two are. And… a very uncool way to divert attention.

me: Yes. Actually, no… you're the first. I lied.

Jyoti: Ahahaha…

me: Lol…

Jyoti: I got the habit in France.

me: France?

Jyoti: I was there for 6 months once. Don't ask how or why.

me: And the French added an 'a' to your haha? :/

Jyoti: That's how they do it in their chats. I guess I was impressionable then. It felt like an elegant way of laughing in text. Became a habit.

me: I smell a French boyfriend.

Jyoti: Weird nose you have.

We were talking about how capitalism won't need people.

me: I like how you refer to capitalism as something external to you, something that you observe.
Whereas this chat wasn't possible without capitalism…
We wouldn't have met without capitalism…
You wouldn't have 3000 followers on Twitter without capitalism…

Jyoti: I see you found me on Twitter!
Anyway, you're mixing capitalism with technology.
Yuri Gagarin happened… Laika… Sputnik… these didn't need capitalism…
Technological advancement is like body function… capitalism is the pathology.
It is not artificial intelligence that is making your company fire people… it is capitalism.
Let's not mix ideas of progress with that which serves the interests of a few fat fucks.
As for me, I've to use the technology that is available to me. Make do in a world that history has made available to me.

me: OK OK OK…

Jyoti: Cool then.

me: Though I wonder if the system that produced Sputnik etc… would it not have arrived at a similar debate… about whether it needed ppl or not.
Anyway…
Tell me, are we at least past the point where you are angry with me?

Jyoti: (Deftly timed question)
I'm willing to ignore my anger.

me: Thanks, I guess.
Though why this largesse, if I may ask?
Jyoti: Because you've possibly read Arendt :)
me: O-kay…
My flight's boarding now btw.
Jyoti: Oh…
You're out of town?
OK OK…
me: Yeah. Talk later. Bye!
Jyoti: Bye!

Wednesday, 13th September. Noon.

Jyoti: Hi
Tell me one thing…
me: Yes?
Jyoti: How did you come across Hannah Arendt's book?
me: Meaning?
Jyoti: What circumstances led you to pick up that book?
What curiosity drove you to it?
Was it a friend?
me: I don't remember. I think it was four-five years back.
Jyoti: Try…
me: What?
Jyoti: To remember…
me: But why is it so important suddenly?

Jyoti: I don't know. Just curious I guess as to how a corporate guy got into such reading.
Reading Amish and all would fit the character better.

me: You really need to tone down the passive–aggressive posturing apropos my reading/ intellect.

Jyoti: Kya yaar… you could see it as proof of me being intrigued by you also, right? (aye hye *apropos*)

me: Is it just that? (see!)

Jyoti: Answer karo chalo…

me: I've always been interested in the second world war. Hitler's crimes. So coming to Eichmann's trial was a natural thing.

Jyoti: Hmm…

me: Yeah, that's it.

Jyoti: Did you like the book?

me: Yes… very much.

Jyoti: So now… given Eichmann is culpable for the mass murder of Jews, why aren't you culpable for hundreds of people losing their jobs?

me: Wow! I sensed this q was around the corner. So is that you circling back to what I do?

Jyoti: Yes.
How you see this is something I'm genuinely curious about.

me: I can think of more questions actually. Counter questions.

Jyoti: OK… go on…

me: So is an American taxpayer guilty considering all that's happening in Syria?

Jyoti: Hmm... Syria?
Not like Eichmann.

me: How?

Jyoti: Eichmann served a murderous regime knowingly and yet he did not bother.

me: But don't the taxpayers also *knowingly* do what they do?

Jyoti: What is it that they do?

me: Pay taxes. They pay for America's wars and misadventures.

Jyoti: Yeah sure but I disagree.
They pay taxes because they have to. They pay to have governance.

me: Citizens are the government. No?

Jyoti: That's putting democracy on a pedestal it has never truly achieved.
(I see you are an expert in what about erg)
(*whataboutery)

me: So are you saying that the responsibility of a passive follower is more when it is a totalitarianism...
But not so much in democracy.

Jyoti: Distance is an important factor.
Eichmann was close, the American is far.

me: That doesn't hold...

Jyoti: OK. Why not?

me: That way drone pilots would have less blame than mercenaries on the ground.
And those who order the drone pilots would have even lesser.

Jyoti: Come on, man, don't jump from the taxpayer to drone pilots.

me: I think my larger point is made.

Jyoti: Which is?

me: If serving totalitarianism is bad, and if today's capitalism or techno-consumerism or whatever you call it is one, then everyone is guilty of compliance.

Jyoti: Wah!

me: I'm serious!

Unless you say that the genocide in Europe was a crime that cannot be compared.

But admitting that would mean that your original question about me becomes invalid…

Ergo… you can't equate me with Eichmann.

Jyoti: Well… you are not a *passive* follower, and certainly not analogous with the American taxpayer.

Anyway, I agree that the Eichmann analogy is harsh.

me: It is.

And Eichmann is guilty, for sure :)

Jyoti: Don't say it with a smiley.

Wednesday, 13th September. Evening.

me: Given Eichmann is guilty, have you realized that you took my umbrella that day and left yours behind?

Jyoti: Eh… did I?

me: Well, yours is much smaller.

Jyoti: It hasn't rained since that day so I didn't realize.

me: Must we meet to exchange umbrellas? How filmy would that be?

Jyoti: The proposal will be considered. I can also buy you a new umbrella from Amazon.

me: I see that you're not averse to buying things on Amazon.

Jyoti: What do you think I am? Some kind of luddite?

me: No… just a hater of monopolistic tendencies :D
Anyway, I prefer the meeting.

Jyoti: Will consider the idea.

Thursday, 14th September. Noon.

me: So, given Eichmann is guilty, have you been able to consider the idea of meeting me again?

Jyoti: Umm…

me: ?

Jyoti: I'm sure it's not the umbrellas.
You mean for the purpose of sex, right?

me: Hahaha…
How about: to know each other better?

Jyoti: To know each other better for what end?

me: I don't know.
Sex?

Jyoti: Ahahaha…

me: What are your plans this evening?
Jyoti: No plans. You're in Mumbai?
me: Yes. Wine at my place?.
Jyoti: Do you have a corkscrew?
me: Actually, no. I had one but someone stole it.
Jyoti: I smell a kleptomaniac girlfriend.
me: Weird nose you have.
I'll step out and buy one.
If you're coming, that is.
Jyoti: I'll buy the wine.
me: Given Eichmann is guilty I'm not interested in Scrabble at all.
Jyoti: I guess I'll just exercise my right to be silent here.
me: It's a nice word, right? Corkscrew.
Jyoti: Dude, chill.

Thursday, 14th September. Evening.

Me: You started yet?
Jyoti: Yes, on my way.
me: Cool.
Jyoti: You know, on my Facebook, I'm seeing ads selling corkscrews and wine glasses and other accessories! That's the kind of work you're doing, right? Apps listening… learning… nudging.
me: Sort of.

Jyoti: It's like this nosy friend who eavesdrops on conversations... and then tries to pitch in with unwanted help.

me: Yes, in a way.
How far are you?

Jyoti: So Facebook knows about our Eichmann conversation, too?
ETA 25 mins.
(Make sure there is no blackout, please)

me: Yes, FB knows. Though I'm sure it can't make head or tail of it.
(Don't worry).

Jyoti: They don't care about conversations they can't monetize.

me: Oh, they'll find a way to do that.
They might show you an ad for the Arendt book.
Next to an ad for Mein Kampf :D

Jyoti: Should we write in jumbled English to avoid these things? I see we are both quite *proper* in chats.

me: That may not work.

Jyoti: Why? It can read jumbled also, you mean?

me: Of course. There is something called natural language processing.
FB machine listens to so many conversations that it can guess the intent and context.
Understands colloquial stuff, common grammar errors, typos.
Now, unless we start talking in code...

Jyoti: So you're saying FB already knows that we might fuck tonight?

me: All doubts have been removed now :D

Jyoti: Ahahaha... yours or FB's?

me: Both... (well, I have to say that my excitement has increased a bit)

Jyoti: (Hope you have the corkscrew)

me: (Is this us talking in code?)

Friday, 15th September. Morning, just after Jyoti leaves my place.

me: Hope you had a good time. I did.

Jyoti: Yes :)
And since you're asking about the sex, let me say that it was decent.

me: When did I ask about the sex!
Anyway, that's good to hear.

Jyoti: But don't be flattered, OK? You can do much better.

me: That's good to know, too.

Jyoti: I think you are flattered.

me: A bit.
I see that you're giving *me* whatever credit there is. And the discourse is only about the improvements *I* could make.

Jyoti: Umm... so you mean to say that I need to make improvements?

me: No… just kidding. Last night was terrific for me. And not just the sex…

Jyoti: Hmm… good to know.
:*

me: Wow, a kiss!

Jyoti: Should I take it back?

me: That's my first ever chatkiss from you.

Jyoti: One can do more than just kissing on chats, you know?

me: Ooo…

Jyoti: Are you the sexting sort?

me: I can't say I don't enjoy it.

Jyoti: For women the icky thing with it is that… once you start it then the man wants it all the time… with every chat.

me: Let us try.
Given Eichmann is guilty, I love biting your nipples. Softly.

Jyoti: Yuck!

me: ?

Jyoti: Let's leave Eichmann out now, please…
Go on… what else do you love doing?

That evening, Jyoti arrives at my place with a small backpack. We spend not just that night but the whole weekend together. On Monday morning, just before leaving my apartment, she announces that she's leaving her toothbrush behind.

We sleep together for the next three nights, too. On Thursday morning, I travel to Bhopal.

Thursday, September 21. While being driven to a restaurant for lunch.

me: Hi

Jyoti: Hey… how are you?

me: I'm good. Going for lunch.

Jyoti: You think of me outside Mumbai too? :)

me: Let's just say I think of you quite a lot these days.

Jyoti: (is not affected by this in the least)

me: I wanted to ask you something…

Jyoti: No no no…

me: !?

Jyoti: I will not marry you. I look at marriage as a hideous instrument of state control, out to create homogeneous, heteronormative entities that are condemned to enmesh themselves in the state*market nexus.

me: Wow… lol! That's intense shit!
I didn't want to talk about marriage though :)
Just wanted to tell you that I talked about you with a colleague.
He's sort of like a friend.

Jyoti: O… kay. You didn't share any saucy details, I hope?

me: Oh come on, don't be crazy.

Jyoti: What did you tell him?

me: That I am seeing someone. You.

There is five minutes of chat silence after this.

Jyoti: That is like saying I'm your girlfriend.
me: Do you mind that?
Jyoti: I don't know.
me: ?
Jyoti: ?
me: You don't know what?
Jyoti: If I want to be mentioned as your girlfriend. Or anyone's for that matter…
But wait… so it's not just the sex for you?
me: Of course not, Jyoti! Fuck, you're cruel.
Jyoti: Am I?
me: So you're saying it's just the sex for you?
Jyoti: No… I like being with you.
Sleeping with you.
Chatting with you.
Whatever.
But this doesn't have to be a relationship.
me: OK.
Jyoti: What? Most men would love the idea.
me: True…
I don't know how I feel now, though.
I mean… sure… it doesn't matter what word is used.
I want it to be more than sex buddy.
And does it mean it's private? Never to be discussed with anyone?

Jyoti: Is it exclusive?

me: !

OK… are you sleeping with someone else?

Jyoti: How could I be sleeping with someone else when I sleep with you every night?

And that's not the point.

me: What's the point?

I would like to know.

Jyoti: I'm asking you whether your conception of what we have assumes exclusive rights over the sexual me?

I'm out of my depth here and, for a moment, I wallow in that familiar feeling that people from small towns can sometimes suffer from – that they're too conservative for big-city folks, that they'll never quite understand them.

me: Yes… I guess it does.

Jyoti: Now *I* don't know how I feel.

me: You told me you broke up with a boyfriend. Was that an open arrangement too?

Jyoti: No.

me: So?

Jyoti: But that was a relationship, you see.

me: What's the point?

Jyoti: Is this a relationship?

me: That's more or less my question to *you*.

Jyoti: Is it really not just sex for you?

me: Why does it feel that this question now is different from this question earlier?

My answer is the same.

Jyoti: Which is?

me: I like being with you. I would like you to be my girlfriend.

Jyoti: Hmm…

Also the fact that you shared it with a corporate dude.

me: Well… I don't know many non-corporate dudes.

Jyoti: He's your age?

me: Older. He's married.

Jyoti: Next thing I know you will ask us to meet them.

Me: If that happens I will ensure there is wine.

Jyoti: Might be interesting to see how corporate dudes bond after office hours.

me: He is a *total* corporate dude, btw. (Sitting right next to me)

Jyoti: And you aren't?

me: Like… he is the one who won't spend a second thinking of the people losing their jobs. He doesn't. I know that.

Jyoti: Hmm…

The archetype, then.

me: Something like that. A decent person. I guess.

Jyoti: Yeah yeah… you guys are all decent people.

And then one finds out more. About how you harass the juniors. Maintain a sexist workplace. Take advantage of women…

me: Can you please keep me out of this generic 'you'?

Jyoti: You are out of it in a way. But you're also deep in it.

me: Well… what you said is so complex it must be true.

Jyoti: It is true.

I think your mild outsiderness exists because you're not from a big city.

Because you *made it till here*

But *making it till here* has also made you cling to what you have.

So you see the contradictions but have trained yourself to look away.

me: Contradictions?

Jyoti: Yes! That the whole shebang is brutal cutthroat inhuman negative… and you aren't really made for it.

That *making it till here* is all fine but what happens after is not very appealing.

me: Weird but… I like when you speculate about me.

Is that how you felt when you quit journalism?

Jyoti: You trying to get back at me now?

me: Did you feel you weren't really made for it?

Jyoti: I have been an investigative journalist. I am made for JOURNALISM. Just that JOURNALISM is a rare thing now.

me: I'm actually driving at a slightly different point.

Jyoti: ?

me: The system may be pathetic, but it's everywhere. Ubiquitous.

That makes taking an ethical stand akin to not participating…

And not participating can leave the person in question feeling inadequate…

Because everyone else is participating.

And there are undeniable material benefits of doing that.

Jyoti: You can say shit like this and still go to work tomorrow? Impressive…

Yes, sometimes I feel inadequate.

And maybe at some point in time I will make a compromise.

A workable compromise.

In which I roam around with the pack but take care not to become a wolf.

me: IMO, that's impossible.

Not becoming the wolf, that is.

Anyway, I'm sorry to have talked about you with my colleague.

Will take care in future.

from: Jyoti S <s_jyoti22@*.com>
to: Saransh Malik <saransh_cr7@*.com>
date: Fri, Sept 22, 2017 at 2:35 AM
subject: Being a girlfriend, and other almost important things

Saransh,

I think I overcomplicated the issue of boyfriend–girlfriend, but I guess you understand that I was speaking from a place of anxiety and insecurity (which is also where this email is coming from, for I'm anxious and insecure about how my response in the chat may have affected your perception of me). It is always scary to accept these labels, for they grant some sort of entitlement to the other party and also remind one of any residual traumas associated with them, especially similar moments with other people – people who left a bitter taste behind. I have been girlfriend to some lousy men and I have been the lousy girlfriend in some cases. But wherever I have been nothing to the other person and the other person has been nothing to me, the question of who amongst us is lousy has never arisen. Simple logic, isn't it? I guess I have come to prefer being nothing rather than being a girlfriend, and so when you said what you said in the chat it came as a bit of a surprise. What I said about exclusivity and whatnot was basically me reacting without knowing how to, or perhaps trying to confirm whether you had just been casual or not, though I guess it was I who came across as super casual, something that you were taken aback by and which possibly made you imagine me as this uber-cosmopolitan chick who has only ever had open relationships and heaps and heaps of polyamory. And although we clarified our positions somewhat I still wanted to write this email to try and tell you that I'm OK being your girlfriend and I'm OK that you are my boyfriend and I'm OK to be your date at your stupid corporate friend's house and that in fact I'm OK being your date each time you are expected to bring a date with you and it's all cool and shit and it's even a little bit awesome if you ask me. Damn!

I think I am also uselessly enigmatic when I call you a mild outsider, while also saying that you are deep in 'it'. I'm extrapolating about you, of course. I may be wrong. I admit, I admit, I admit. But what I mean is simply that despite having worked through your twenties you have managed to not be completely enmeshed in corporate culture and the cutthroat-y values it demands of all participants. You are sensitive in general and somewhat interested in the ethical issues w.r.t. your participation in a specific version of the capital-vs-labour narrative. Yet you have allowed yourself to believe in your total dependence on the system simply because your environment has convinced you that you need the money, the security, the routine, the alignment, the I-do-it-because-it's-done thing. It is actually a completely rational position and I know that it is I who is the unreasonable one, even the violent one, for I harp upon a contradiction in you which is in fact the contradiction implicit in twenty-first century life, and if I'm blaming you for being in 'it' then what exactly is it that I'm blaming you for? I have no locus standi here. I, too, am living a different version of the same contradiction. I have quit journalism but I may go back to it. I am writing a children's book and when I am done with it, I will seek a corporate publisher and be very happy if the most well-established house takes my book up for a big sum. And isn't everything I consume also made industrially, underwritten by some or other exploitative process? And so, is it really prudent to focalize on any particular instance of exploitation or discrimination or tech-ruination or whatnot, for if these things are everywhere and happening all the time, if violence to each other is the only way humans can be humans, if it is only the modality of violence that changes, if dystopia is the only possible culmination of our techno-capitalist progress and no power is powerful enough to avert it, then isn't the only rational choice the one in which you just choose to go about things with silence? Which is to say, find a bed, fuck, sleep, wake up, and then pass those ten hours at work? I think that's what you do and are, to some degree, aware of doing, and although I have my issues with that, I'm aware that I'm wrong to have those issues.

And there is no sarcasm in the above paragraph. None.

One request I have is that we refrain from employing the 'given Eichmann is guilty' line of conversation ever again. It is vulgar and disrespectful. I know that I was the one who brought it in, who tried to establish the equivalence, but I'm well aware that there is no equivalence possible between that man's crimes and the crimes that you are 'arguably' committing in your job. The mere suggestion of it makes me feel like a horrible person and on top of that we have made it a bit of a private joke whose privacy and hilarity are both problematic if we really pause and think about it. *So what* if we are Indians and know the Holocaust only through great Hollywood movies? We know enough to know that that crime must not be relativized.

Conversely, simultaneously, contradictorily, Jyoti-ly, I would like it to be clear that in my mind there is no way that you are completely without blame. You are to blame, most definitely you are. Your wrongdoing is palatable only because this sort of thing has been so normalized, because we are all guilty in one way or another. But think of those branch executives who will lose their jobs. They are bound to undergo a major disruption in their lives, and I'm sure that back in your office they are spoken of not as people but as a single number that needs to be deleted from some Excel spreadsheet. The standard argument is often that irrelevance caused by technological advancement forces people to seek higher skills, that it allows people to be free from what is usually called drudgery, that progress takes place through such upheavals – but these statements are true only at the macro level and cannot conceal how colossally indifferent the powers that be are w.r.t. the pain of any single individual who is directly affected by this – what should we call it? – tyrannical? – action. Hundreds of people will lose their jobs and you will probably be well-rewarded when that happens and the company will of course save crores of rupees, which might allow them to expand in other operations and therefore generate employment elsewhere, and so it is possible that an equal number of people will get jobs after your success. I get all that. But it is only with a hopelessly macro-utilitarian view of the world that we can justify this sort of game. Those who lose their jobs aren't the ones who later on get the new job. That's a fact and you know it and everyone knows it. The people who lose their jobs will just have to scrounge elsewhere. Nothing will reduce their suffering, and nothing will mitigate the fact that you are party to creating that suffering. But since you cannot escape inflicting this suffering upon them, perhaps you should suffer a bit yourself by feeling guilty in the knowledge that you have done or are going to do some harm.

Also, a question that I think you must think about: would you change this if you somehow, miraculously, got a chance?

Je t'embrasse.

Jyoti

I came back to Mumbai late at night on Thursday, though much before Jyoti wrote her email.

Friday, September 22. Morning.

me: Hey

Read your email.

You wrote quite a bit.

I mean you wrote a long email :)

I have read it three times, in fact.
Very poorly written… Haha
You are abject with punctuation.
:)

I'm writing this as I get ready for work, knowing that Jyoti isn't up yet.

me: I guess you aren't up yet.
me: I'll answer the email. Going to work now.
I google translated je t'embrasse. Lovely.

Evening. Before leaving office for home.

me: Hey…
How are you?

Jyoti has read my messages from the morning. But she hasn't replied. Even now, she takes fifteen minutes before answering.

Jyoti: Hey sorry I was out doing a bit of grocery…
Should I come? You wanted us to watch that superhero movie tonight?
me: Yes, come.
Hey, I'm sorry I couldn't answer your email
I didn't get the time at work.
Jyoti: It's fine.
me: No I mean I intend to…
Just that I feel I need more time to do justice to it.

It's so well-thought and so well-written…

Jyoti: Really?

You said otherwise…

me: Yes, I was goofing. But, no, it's really good.

The ideas…

Jyoti: Hey you really don't have to worry about answering me…

We can talk.

me: No, I think I need to.

Jyoti: What?

me: The writing… I mean, I need to write a response to you.

Jyoti: ?

me: Because I think writing will help me know what I think abt things…

With writing there is more time to articulate things.

I will write to you.

Jyoti: I understand.

Guess that's why I wrote the email in the first place. To articulate things better.

Sorry if it's overwhelmed you.

me: I don't know. I guess it has… But the Eichmann point is correct. I agree completely :)

Jyoti: Hmm…

me: And hey I will answer that email for sure…

Jyoti: OK. I will await the answer but no pressure.

ZEPPELIN

IN THE SECOND WEEK OF OCTOBER, MITESH AND I TRAVEL to Nashik by road. We opt for an overnight stay in the city at a three-star hotel where my room's toilet gives off a rancid smell despite looking spotlessly clean. In the evening we drink whiskey with soda in Mitesh's room. After some time, Mitesh opens up and starts talking about his married life. 'Having a kid is a disaster for your sex life,' he declares between heavy sighs. He then asks me how things are 'progressing' with Jyoti. I respond with a plain 'all good'. Our attention then shifts to the muted TV, where a Hindi news channel shows a heated debate with JNU student Kanhaiya Kumar as one of the participants. Mitesh abuses Kumar and starts talking about the JNU sedition row. He wishes the harshest punishment on Kumar and 'all the haraami anti-nationals' named in connection. I point out how the crisis seems to be fabricated, and that nobody has been named in any chargesheet yet. This fact is not relevant for Mitesh; he claims to know a lot of things about the culture inside JNU, which is funny because I don't think he's even visited

Delhi more than a couple of times in his life. I keep my disagreements silent and that allows Mitesh to rant about JNU and several other anti-national and anti-Hindu things for long. It is only when my silence begins to bore him that he changes the topic. He asks me how things are progressing with Jyoti. I remind him that he's already asked me the question. Then, after a pause, he stutteringly invites me and Jyoti to his apartment for a Sunday lunch. 'Jyoti must come,' he insists. I accept reluctantly with the disclaimer that Jyoti might have other plans that day.

At around 7 a.m. the next morning we start the journey back to Mumbai in the car assigned to us. We move at a good speed. Mitesh complains about the tetchy sleep he had the previous night. At some point in the journey, when the only sound inside the air-conditioned car is of its tyres whooshing over the highway, Mitesh falls asleep; his light snoring mixes with the sound of the tyres. To avoid doing the same (according to me, both of us sleeping will make the driver reckless), I ping Jyoti. I remind her about my proposal for spending the Diwali week in Goa, something that I had brought up with her a couple of days ago. She ignores the Goa mention. In fact, with what she sends me as reply, my hopes for an easy, tripping conversation are quashed. It is a news item, apparently from the previous day, about the rape of a minor in Punjab. Rape and murder. After sharing the news link, Jyoti complains that she can't work on her children's book, not because she cannot write per se but because she is questioning her reasons for writing what she is writing. What use is it to write a book for children in this world, she asks, and although the question is posed to me it is obvious that I am not required to answer. I still type in some plain words about how every good book will improve a small part of the future, how each tiny effort has value, how the world is big and our actions can only be small, but I'm not sure I believe the words myself, and even as I send them to her I know that they will provide little solace, if any, which is confirmed when Jyoti only responds with a 'Hmm…' We are silent for a few minutes after that. She then asks, again herself more than me, that if she had to write a book why did she end up wanting to write a children's book. She doesn't have children, doesn't plan to have any, doesn't even have nephews or nieces. 'Is loving children in the abstract a qualification enough?' she writes. And I realize that this is a question that I, too, have wanted to ask Jyoti. I don't say anything in response, not for a few minutes at least. Then I type in a neutral 'We will talk', signalling an end to the chat, and move on to searching for the horrible news myself.

We enter the city just before noon. The driver asks us where we want to go and we give him coordinates to the office. 'I know where Bansal Towers is, sir,' the driver says, 'I have an account with Bansal bank.' He grins and looks into the rear-view mirror, seeking a reaction from us. We don't give him any.

At a red light in Powai, Mitesh says, 'I think we can stop with the branch visits now.' He is rubbing and pressing his eyes with his fingers, as if to squeeze the fatigue out of them.

'If there are any more anomalies left we will just have to live with them.'

In the Nashik branch office, too, we discovered an anomaly. It was related to life insurance sales to Non-Resident Indians (NRIs). Whenever the two LOEs in Nashik receive an NRI's insurance application, they insist on checking the latest immigration stamps on the customer's passport. They then compare the customer's period of stay in the country to the date on which the insurance application was submitted on iSmart. According to them, if the iSmart date is the date on which the sales guy completed the act of selling to the customer (a fair assumption), then it follows that the customer should have been in India on that date. For a discrepancy on this front (the iSmart date not falling between the customer's period of stay in India), or for the sales guy's inability to produce a photocopy of the immigration stamps on the customer's passport, the LOEs refuse to receipt the case till the sales guy provides an email approval by the Zonal Sales Head.

The two LOEs appeared very proud while telling us all this. We appreciated it effusively before them, of course. It did sound like an incredibly intelligent process, targeted at possibly fraudulent sales activities in NRI cases, which tend to be high-risk for the company. After the interviews we called George to check about the practice. George told us that to his knowledge no such check for an NRI customer's immigration dates exists elsewhere. He acknowledged that the process was incredibly smart. But for us this meant that the two LOEs in Nashik were just too intelligent. Because in our project, locally brewed intelligence is called an anomaly.

'How long till we start asking LOEs to leave the company?' I ask Mitesh. We are next to the big Powai lake in which, people believe, there exists a bunch of crocodiles.

'It will take some time, for…' Mitesh says, rolling down his window and lighting a cigarette, '… for right now, we need to incorporate the anomaly identifiers in the training data sets. That will take some time. Then we monitor the test results for a couple of weeks. Maybe more.'

'Makes sense,' I say. The testing data he is talking about is the data that is fed to the machine. The whole idea of finding anomalies was to exclude them from the learning process so that the machine did not ascribe arbitrary relationships between variables in incoming data – in other words, it was done to save the machine from confusing itself at the beginning, something that had happened during our first iteration. Later, when we understand the anomalies well enough ourselves – which is to say, when HO has decided what to do in each scenario – we will label the instances properly and include them as well.

'But you know this from the iBlink project plan,' Mitesh points out, sharing the lit cigarette with me. 'I'm sure you do. You're the one who made it.'

'Yes, yes,' I say, taking a puff. 'But the project plan doesn't specify exactly when the company starts firing people. So I thought I'd ask you.'

'Of course, it doesn't,' Mitesh says. 'How could it? I don't think we will be able to do that, the firing-people part, until the financial year ends. Hence nothing until the end of March.'

This confirms what I had already sensed. It is October now and the SPG will be ready with the functionality only towards the end of December. From January, the last quarter of the financial year will start. Firing people in the last quarter could have repercussions, especially as nearly 60 per cent of the overall annual business is done during these last three months (people recall insurance's tax-saving properties only towards the end of the financial year, flocking to the same insurance agents they'd been scampering away from earlier in the year). What if the second iteration of iBlink also has issues? The company wouldn't want to deal with faulty automation after having dismantled the manual infrastructure.

'So the management will wait until April?' I ask Mitesh, handing back the cigarette to him.

'Yes,' he says. 'But because of the delay now they might speed things up then. I guess they will wipe out everybody inside of a month.' He has a hint of a smile on his face as he says this. I nod in response, then cough once.

Our car pierces an orchestra of honking at a big signal and turns to join the Western Express Highway. As it speeds up, Mitesh gets distracted with the view outside the window. I unlock my phone's screen and re-read the chat with Jyoti.

One atrocity reminds me of another, and I again begin to obsess over the death of Alan Kurdi. More than my mind's eye seeing flashes of his dead body, what now affects me more deeply is the knowledge of the event itself, the event of his death. I feel the helplessness of not being able to prevent it. An absurd feeling, yes – I wasn't there, I couldn't have done anything; his death is a calamity unrelated to my existence. Jyoti, I understand, must have felt something like this while reading the horrific news today. Words from the email she wrote to me a few days ago come back to me: *You should suffer a bit yourself… by feeling guilty*.

I have read the email countless times. When alone at home, I have read parts of it aloud to myself. Seated inside Zepellin, I have scrolled through it as others around me peered into their laptops. On recent branch visits, I have sneakily read lines of it at airport lounges, during car rides, even while waiting for to-be-interviewed LOEs in the 'Take a Deep Breath Room'. Each time I read the email, in part or fully, a desire to assimilate its words into myself, into some definition of my being, is something I feel strongly. No one has written to me, about me, like this before. But despite the promise to answer it, I have not been able to do so. I guess I dread that any response will convince Jyoti of my banality, the banality of a conformist. It must already be apparent, I know, but to spell it out in words is something I would rather dodge. Online chats about those very same ideas are fine, face-to-face conversations are fine, even silence is fine, for all these are wrapped in an atmosphere of spontaneity, but an email, a letter – a concentrate of my thoughts and feelings – is something altogether different. What if the concentrate comes out too bland?

The car stops outside the second gate of Bansal Tower. As we step out and as Mitesh pays the driver in cash, I take a few more moments with my thoughts, and try to foster what Jyoti's email intended to – a pang of specific guilt, uniquely related to my existence, to the work that I have done and I am doing and I will do inside this building. But I am not successful. I feel only a diffused guilt that, I immediately realize, is essentially second-hand – borne out of witnessing from an always-comfortable distance the all-too-common atrocities of the world. The Punjabi kid's rape and murder, like Alan Kurdi's drowning. But why is this diffused guilt not as all-too-common as its causes are? Shouldn't everyone in the world at least have this feeling to some degree? And what must this feeling lead to? What must one – and everyone – do about it?

Inside Zepellin, two old iSmart-related charts are taken off the wall and new ones are put up in their place. On these, we stick Post-its, each specifying an anomaly that we have discovered for iBlink. There are 108 anomalies in all (anomalies can combine with each other and produce a great number of actual scenarios), and the task of putting them up takes more than an hour. When we are done, we clap, hug each other, utter some silly jokes. For lunch, we order pizzas.

After lunch, I bump into Rizwan at the water cooler. We talk about how tasty the pizzas were, and how it might be difficult to stay awake in the next meeting, an SPG-only discussion about the underwriting project proposed by Brahma. Rizwan takes a step closer to me and starts talking in a conspiratorial voice: 'Poonam is the one taking charge of this meeting. Trained as an underwriter and all, that's why. That's Unni's logic. But the funny thing is: she didn't want to do it. Did you know that? No? You know what she told George? She said, "Let's see if this works on the LOEs first." She doesn't like what it will do to underwriters, you see.' I don't know why Rizwan is telling me this; just out of a need to gossip, maybe. I nod towards him and finish drinking my glass of water.

In the next five minutes, all the SPG members gather inside the Zepellin. Poonam connects her laptop to the TV's display. She is supposed to tell us about the as-is underwriting process and give initial ideas on the to-be process, with the journey from as-is to to-be of course considered in the light of what the Brahma people had proposed. Mitesh, George and I sit on one side of the table. Rizwan, Ankita and Sayantan are on the other side. The lights have been switched off but the screen's glow is such that, being the farthest from it, I can see everyone's faces clearly.

Poonam starts. Her presentation is titled *Taking Underwriting to the Next Level*. On the first slide itself she feels the need to emphasize her intention to discuss the potential challenges associated with the endeavour. On the third slide, she informs us that, like with all life insurance companies, a considerable percentage of our mortality risk –

the risk of a customer dying during the policy tenure and of the company thus having to pay the claim amount – is in fact *re*insured, that is, sold to companies like Swiss Re, Munich Re, Hannover Re, et cetera, global powerhouses whose raison d'être is precisely this sort of risk buying. 'It follows that just as we are interested to know about the lifestyles of our customers, our reinsurance partners are interested in our lifestyles,' Poonam quips. 'So, what is our lifestyle?'

'The decisions we make regarding which customers we will insure and which ones we will deny,' Mitesh answers.

'Exactly,' says Poonam. 'These are what we call underwriting practices. Now, it is without question that any changes in our underwriting practices need to add to and not subtract from the confidence of the reinsurers. Just as for us, it is better if all our customers start eating greens and go jogging every morning.'

Everyone in the room laughs. I laugh, too, though I feel the analogy to be a bit stretched.

'What the members of this room do not know, however – and I should have mentioned this in front of the Brahma guys when they were here in September – is that, even today, more than 60 per cent of our cases *are* automated,' Poonam says. She then pauses and spreads her arms for effect. It's like her task here is already over; it's like she is asking us, her fellow SPG members, to consider the existing automation percentage as the highest possible and shift our attention elsewhere. The 60 per cent number is in fact only mildly surprising, but Poonam's satisfaction in communicating it is bizarre. 'I repeat, no human underwriter looks at 60 per cent of the applications,' she carries on. 'The application data passes straight through a rule engine software that executes our underwriting algorithm. The algorithm is very strong. Robust. And it is not, as that Brahma guy said, a product of emotion. It is the sum of learnings from years of experience. It undergoes changes every now and then, of course. There is an underwriting committee that deliberates and decides on each change. But, yes, three out of five of our applications are straight-through. Which is to say that only two out of five cases are seen by underwriters.'

'It's a bunch of old rules, Poonam,' Mitesh says with a drawl. There is no way Poonam's comfort regarding the current process is not apparent to him.

Poonam doesn't respond to Mitesh; instead, she moves to the next slide, which shows two pictures connected through multiple arrow-headed lines. The picture on the left is of a white man holding a phone; the one on the right is of a black woman holding a phone. The picture on the left is titled Insurance Underwriter; the one on the right is titled Reinsurer Risk Assessor. Each connecting line is topped with some text and a sequence number.

'As you can see,' Poonam says, 'for some of the manually underwritten applications – the two out of five, ones that the rule engine software identifies as potentially risky – there can be a good degree of consultation or negotiation or haggling, whatever you want to call it, between the insurance company's underwriters and the risk assessors of the reinsurance company.'

'So you're saying that things are subjective,' Ankita says, her right hand's palm moving as if it were practicing a diminutive karate move in slow-motion.

'Yes, but that in itself means nothing,' says Poonam. 'Over the years, underwriting decisions for similar customer profiles can be completely different. This can be due to variance in human decision-making, or due to shifts in the underwriting philosophy of the company. The shifts are usually an outcome of changes in the reinsurer contract terms.'

'Are these calls transcribed?' I ask.

'Which ones? Poonam asks.

'The ones between our underwriter and the reinsurance guy,' I clarify.

Poonam chuckles. 'No. These two people can talk about everything under the sun before they discuss the specifics of an application. You see, depending on the relationship with our underwriter, the risk assessor may even reveal information about how a competitor's underwriters are looking at the same customer's case. This is all, of course, informal. Maybe even illegal. But all very useful. This will stop if we start recording the calls.'

'Have the instances of reinsurer-initiated changes in our underwriting rules been documented?' I ask.

'The history of changes in the rule engine is maintained, but that will largely give information about the 60 per cent of cases that are already automated,' offers Poonam. 'How human underwriting has changed over time is not documented.'

'Thanks, I thought so,' I say, knocking the table with my knuckles twice. If we go by what Poonam has said, the science behind the processing of 40 per cent of insurance applications in BLIC is actually an art. Or a black box that cannot be read.

Mitesh also realizes this as I do, something made amply clear by how he places his palm on his forehead. Rizwan has perhaps been in on it since the beginning. It is he who speaks aloud for the benefit of the rest. 'So, Poonam, you're saying that there will be anomalies in the human underwriting data sets.'

'Absolutely, yes,' says Poonam.

'So we can interview the underwriters,' suggests Mitesh, 'just as we did with the LOEs. There are only forty of them, anyway. And all of them are at the HO. We won't even need to travel. We could finish it in two weeks.'

'Underwriters are the executors of the risk philosophy of the company, Mitesh. Being secretive about their jobs is the ethos. Besides, they are HO employees. They won't fall for the manipulations of a guidebook for sure,' answers Poonam.

George suddenly comes alive. 'You're saying that the LOEs are stupid? That it was easy to get answers out of them? That it was easy to make the LIFE guide?'

'I'm not calling anyone stupid,' says Poonam.

'Chill, man,' I tell George, patting him on the shoulder.

Poonam continues: 'Interviewing won't work, but we can collect the information we need slowly, automatically... say... in three-four years.' She moves on to the next slide, which contains a series of bullet points. 'During that period our operating model for this project,' she gestures towards the slide, 'will need to involve a combination of machines and humans. Let the machine suggest a decision… let the human accept it or reverse it… let the machine then learn from the human action. Let the machine essentially act as a guide to the human underwriter, a second opinion kind of thing.'

This man–machine collaboration is a new idea. We never considered it in the LOE project. There, even during the learning phase, we are never going to show the machine's decision to the LOE. The machine will surreptitiously learn from the variance between its decision and the LOE's decision until it is ready to take over completely. What Poonam is suggesting for the underwriting project is a model where the machine and the human collaborate to decide on applications.

'So you're saying it will take years for the machine to be ready to make the final decision?' Mitesh asks anxiously.

'If ever,' Poonam says. 'Changes in the company's risk strategy will mean that we will always need a rule box that we can explicitly configure for managing the 60 per cent automated cases. For the manual cases, training people is still faster than training machines. Also, what about the wrong decisions? Let me be clear: we *cannot* afford to make a wrong decision at the underwriting stage. In the LOE project things are different because decisions taken at the branch can always be reversed in the HO. The risk of the machine making a bad decision in the LOE project is not… how do you say… exis...'

'Existential,' I say.

'Yes, existential!' Poonam says. 'Thanks.'

'You're welcome. Though you are wrong about one thing here,' I say. 'Training people is not faster than training machines.'

'Maybe so, but my point is also that people take blame for mistakes,' Poonam says with a hard smile, 'and a machine can never do that.'

Poonam's smile doesn't save the room from constricting a bit, with everyone's head simultaneously buzzing with responses to her line of argument.

Mitesh starts. 'Which error is riskier? A machine saying Yes wrongly? Or a machine saying No wrongly? Which decision, if faulty, harms the company more? I guess what I'm asking is which mistake is *more* existential?'

'A machine saying Yes wrongly,' George announces. 'What if the machine says Yes to a guy who has serious health issues?'

'We don't want bad risk on our books,' Ankita adds, her confidence conveying that she has no idea how vapid her contribution is.

'That's why I said that humans will be needed,' Poonam quips, 'because, of course, a majority of our cases *are* a Yes. And it is always going to be like this. So to find a single error means that all the machine-Yes cases will need to pass through human eyes. The point I want to make is: 60 per cent of our cases don't need the intelligent machine, and the remaining 40 per cent of cases cannot be automated with *any* machine.'

'That's self-defeating,' says Mitesh sharply. 'That's an argument that will lead us towards retaining the entire underwriting team. That's like saying, do nothing. Where is your bias for action, Poonam?'

'I'm sorry to disappoint you, Mitesh,' Poonam says, again with her arms spread, 'but that's how it is.'

I note Mitesh's semantics: failure to fire people=self-defeating. His argument with Poonam doesn't interest me. It is clear that the problem needs to be looked at differently, something that the room's emotional charge – the abrupt silences, the aggressive turn in tones – is unlikely to allow right now.

'We could perhaps aim for machine-No applications in the 40 per cent lot to not be checked by a human,' Poonam says, drawing attention to another bullet point on her slide. 'That would be about 5 to 7 per cent of our overall number of cases. That could help reduce manpower by a bit.'

What Poonam is suggesting would probably allow us to fire two people, if at all. Mitesh gives a frustrated shake of the head and clicks his ballpoint pen's button multiple times. Ankita makes eye contact with me and purses her lips. George shifts in his chair, the expression on his face making me fear that he is holding back a fart. Rizwan taps the pantry service number on the speakerphone and orders some coffee. The unsaid question in everyone's mind is whether Poonam is being objective or if she is being smart and trying to save her erstwhile colleagues.

My phone starts vibrating. The call is not from an identified contact though I am convinced that the number on display is the same number that had called me about a month ago at an awkward moment. At least the last four digits are the same. I excuse myself and walk out of Zepellin. By now the vibration has stopped. I proceed towards the break-out area and dial back on the missed call.

'Hello.'

'Hello, sir. This Vijayalaxmi, sir.'

'Yes… Hi, Vijayalaxmi. How are you? I'm sorry we could not talk properly the last time you called.'

'That is not a problem, sir. That is not a problem.'

A pause. I sense Vijayalaxmi is hesitating. 'So, Vijayalaxmi, how can I help you?'

'Actually I want help only, sir.'

'Yes, go on. What is it that you need help with?'

'I want transfer to Mumbai, sir,' she says.

'Transfer to Mumbai?' I ask in disbelief. Then, after taking a moment to put an empty cup beneath the coffee dispenser, 'Why?'

'My husband is in Mumbai, sir,' Vijayalaxmi says. 'Now he is in Mumbai for more than six months.'

So what can I do? I think. My coffee is ready. 'Have you discussed this with your boss?' I ask her.

'Yes, sir,' she replies, 'but he is saying that for LOE from Hyderabad there is no chance going to Mumbai.'

I take a sip of the coffee, lick the froth off my lips. 'He is probably right, Vijayalaxmi,' I say.

'But who can make the chance, sir?'

'I didn't get you.'

'I am saying… who can make it possible, sir, for LOE from Hyderabad to go to Mumbai? I think someone from HO can help, sir.'

'You're probably right,' I say. 'But I'm not the right person in HO to help you with this. You should find someone in HR, maybe.'

'I write to HR, sir,' she answers immediately. 'I write to HR but they not write back. Never write back.'

'Hmm,' I take a sip of the coffee and wonder if I'm needed in Zepellin. Then I hear a different sort of sound on the phone, as if Vijayalaxmi is crying at the other end. 'Vijayalaxmi?'

'Sir…' she says, clearly sniffling. 'Sir… actually my husband is lost… missing. He go Mumbai six months ago. Then for previous four months he not picking up phone. No message also. Police in my city is not showing interest. Saying he found another woman. I want to go to Mumbai to find him. But without job I cannot do finding more than one week, two week.'

She starts to sound like she's hyperventilating or crying violently. I don't know what to say to her. It now makes sense why she took my number during the Hyderabad visit. Finding a new job in a new city will be difficult for her; she wants to take her chances inside BLIC.

'Sir, George sir moved from Chennai to Mumbai,' she reminds me between hiccups.

'George is a senior person, Vijayalaxmi. And he was required for HO work.'

'I understand,' she says, 'but can you please check, sir? At least please check.'

'OK, I'll check if there is a provision for a transfer like this,' I say. After a second I add, 'best of luck,' though it feels wrong to say those words.

'Thank you, sir.'

She disconnects the call and I dump my half-filled coffee cup in the sink. The conversation has left a bad taste in my mouth. As I walk towards Zepellin, I am weighed down by the knowledge that irrespective of whether Vijayalaxmi is a LOE in Hyderabad or Mumbai, there are only a few months left for her in BLIC. After April, processing the anomalous scenarios (the ones the machine won't decide on) will still require some LOE-type manpower in HO. But that's work for five people, max. And that too only for three to four months.

Inside Zepellin I find Poonam talking about a conference that she had attended recently. The other people in the room seem bored by now (Mitesh is deep into his phone). Poonam nevertheless speaks about something called 'fraud analytics', which according to her is a way to assign to each incoming insurance application a numeric probability of turning into a fraudulent claim in the future, thereby enabling underwriters to pay more attention to suspect cases at the time of entry itself. It makes sense to me. To George, however, the term *fraud analytics* becomes a joke unto itself. When she hears him repeat the words disparagingly, Poonam raises her voice: 'Fraud analytics is going to be very very valuable. Definitely more compared to our current fancy of reducing manpower without understanding the underlying processes.' Hearing this, Mitesh looks up from his phone, only to find an expression of fortitude on Poonam's face. I feel some admiration for Poonam, even though I am convinced that more than empathy for fellow underwriters, it is her own pride in her earlier profession that is making her do what she is doing. Both her fortitude and my admiration are silly, of course. I already know that the word *fancy* will have some repercussions.

'Thank you, Poonam,' Mitesh says coldly. 'We should definitely deliberate upon the risks that you have highlighted. And we should definitely look at the other alternatives that you have suggested.' He turns to look away from her, towards me and George, and then adds, 'I insist, however, that we do not abandon the original idea.'

'Exactly, Mitesh,' George says in an aggrieved manner, 'there is a difference between saying that we have AI-powered underwriting with zero human intervention and saying that we try to use tech to improve human underwriting. Which one sounds better, eh?' He prods each member of the room with his racy, protuberant eyes. 'Which one sounds more powerful? The first one sounds more powerful, I tell you. That's the one we have to pursue.'

'What do you think, Saransh?' Mitesh asks me.

I give it a few seconds only to find myself distracted by a mixture of thoughts – my chat with Jyoti, questions of guilt, Vijayalaxmi's request a few minutes ago. 'I need to absorb what Poonam has shared,' I say. Not satisfied with my answer, Mitesh probes Ankita with raised eyebrows. She starts to say something, but I don't wait to listen to her; excusing myself, I step out of the room again.

I walk to a different zone in the office, the one where the HR department sits. There I approach a specific cubicle, the one belonging to Manpreet, who is the HR person I find the most easy to talk to. I catch her peering into her laptop in a posture that must be suicidal for any spine in the world.

'Hi,' I say.

She turns. 'Oh wow! How come, yaar, how come? How come an SPG member has abandoned the den to talk to us lesser mortals?'

'I want to know about the company's transfer policy,' I say, coming straight to the point.

'Ha…' Manpreet laughs heartily. 'Reminds me of that movie scene… in which this guy says, "I want to know the procedure to change the hostel room"… so all is not well in paradise, eh?'

'No no… it's not for me.'

'You want to send someone else to a remote grave?'

'Oh, stop with the jokes, Manpreet,' I say. 'I just want to know if you've access to any written policy regarding transfers?'

'Of course, I do,' she says. 'It's a simple policy. There isn't much to read.'

'What does it say?'

'Well, broadly speaking, employees may be transferred from one location to another by company order… or… through a formal transfer application made by the employee in which he or she provides details of the specific circumstances, personal or political or Biblical, yeah, due to which he or she seeks the said transfer. In the second case, a transfers' committee evaluates the application and has to respond with a yes or a no within three months. The committee actually exists, in case you were wondering.'

'I'm sure it exists. Can a LOE file an application for transfer?'

'What?'

'Can a LOE seek a transfer?'

'Umm… technically, yes. Since they are employees like you and me. But the caveat is that an employee-initiated transfer cannot lead to a promotion or any sort of expansion in the employee's scope of work. It cannot lead to any sort of advancement, you see.'

'So, essentially a LOE…'

'… will be transferred as a LOE,' Manpreet completes my sentence. 'Which is a bit weird because the job description itself says *Local*. Who are you asking for, dude?'

'Well… some LOE,' I say. 'She has good reasons to move to Mumbai.'

'We typically don't communicate the transfer policy, and definitely not to that crowd. So be discreet,' Manpreet says.

'That crowd?'

'Yes. They will then keep asking for transfers, no? The Kolkata guy will want to move to Asansol, the Navi Mumbai guy to Thane, the Haridwar guy to Meerut, and so on and so forth… Frankly, I don't think we've ever received a transfer request from a LOE.' She moves closer to me to say the next bit: 'It will be a nightmare for us, man. They're too many.'

'Oh, don't worry about being discreet,' I say. 'I'm only going to tell that one LOE, and I'm going to make it sound like it's a secret, like it's an exception being created only for her.'

'What will sound like a secret?' It is Mitesh speaking from behind me. 'I was looking for you, Saransh. Hi, Manpreet.'

'*Two* guys from the SPG! My god, today is my big day.' Manpreet looks up to the ceiling and blinks a few times.

'Chal, let's go for a smoke,' Mitesh says to me. 'I bummed a couple from a guy in underwriting.'

'All right. Thanks, Manpreet.'

'No problem,' Manpreet says. 'I'm anyway going to need a moment to recover from the fact that two SPG guys walked up to *my* cubicle. What's the fucking date today? I need to mark it. Can I ask for a selfie?'

'You must try your hand at comedy, you know,' I say.

Mitesh and I walk out of the seating zone and into the lobby area where we call for the lift. Inside the lift, Mitesh, speaking in a hushed tone, says, 'Poonam's presentation is practically her saying *I can't do it, I won't do it, do whatever the fuck you guys want*. Is the drive to reduce manpower fancy?'

'I think she meant fanciful,' I say.

Mitesh rolls his eyes and says, 'Fucking bitch.'

On the ground floor, we walk towards the smoking area behind the two-wheeler parking lot. Stunned by the words Mitesh has used for Poonam, I take a moment to look towards him walking next to me – pressing his tie against his tummy, scrolling through something on his phone, licking his lips, eager for the cigarette he has bummed from someone he wants to be jobless. How adroit he is with his own conscience. There is a nakedness in him, to him – a vulgarity that hides below the professional facade, but which can bare its head every now and then. Guilt, it hits me then, is the absence of vulgarity. Or maybe vulgarity is the absence of guilt.

The smoking area smells of a million cigarettes. This time last year, an employee from Bansal Bank had died here of cardiac arrest. One moment he was smoking his Benson & Hedges, the very next he was prone on the floor. 'As dead as the cigarette butts around him,' people got used to saying. Since then, the good folks in admin have added a defibrillator to the area, a gesture which has invited innumerable witticisms, all filled with the sort of resigned irony that is the hallmark of regular smokers. Some people make it a point to crush their cigarette butts against the glass box behind which the defibrillator rests.

'What do you think?' Mitesh asks while handing me a cigarette and lighting his.

'About what?'

'About what? About the underwriting project.'

'You need to be practical, Mitesh. You can't use machine learning just because you want to fire people. Or you can't fire people just because you want to use machine learning. I don't know how your mind works. But whichever way you're thinking about it, it's wrong. Sixty per cent of underwriting is already automated and that's a fact we can't ignore. Our play is limited here.'

'Yes, I know that,' Mitesh says.

'The Brahma guy… Raju… all his gyan about man-made algorithms being emotional and whatnot… There is more logic in a saas-bahu serial than that shit he threw at us.'

'What do you expect, the Brahma guys have an interest in calling our current system crap,' says Mitesh.

'…'

'Poonam revealed something interesting, you know.'

'What?'

'That the rule engine software that they use for the 60 per cent automation… that's a system provided by a reinsurer.'

'Oh.'

'Yeah.'

'Which means the reinsurers have a commercial interest in things not changing.'

'Exactly.'

'Which means we'll have to be careful, Mitesh. One of the main things in Poonam's presentation today… if you saw what I saw… was that our relationship with reinsurers is sacrosanct. It cannot be threatened by any decisions we make with regards to AI-based automation. A nuanced problem statement is emerging here, Mitesh. More nuanced than saying that I want everyone out of their jobs.'

Mitesh tries to laugh, but ends up coughing out the smoke in his lungs. 'What is this nuanced problem statement, sir?'

'That we use AI to *significantly* increase the automation from 60 per cent *without* increasing the risk to the company or alienating the reinsurers.'

'Aaah,' Mitesh says, stretching the syllable to ensure that I know I have said something painfully obvious.

I take a long drag off the cigarette and hold it in for the few seconds in which what needs to be done becomes clear to me. I flick the ash to the floor and start.

'Keep the reinsurer's system. Continue using it to achieve 60 per cent automation. Use AI for the rest. Now, think of it – changes in the way underwriting is done will always affect applications that are at the border between a Yes-decision and a No-decision. Changes mean that the border shifts slightly, yeah? But that doesn't mean we can't make out the countries. What Poonam has done today is that she's got us too worried about border issues. "What if there is an error? What if a No becomes a Yes?" Let's ignore that border. Let's ignore the border issues. The training data set for the machine that we make should consist of all applications that went to underwriters and in which the underwriters did not bat an eyelid in saying Yes. Basically, cases that are deep in the territory of Yes and far from the border of Yes and No. And therefore, not impacted by any changes in underwriting practices over time.'

'How do we find these cases?' Mitesh asks.

'We will have to find a proxy that we already measure or know of,' I say, taking another long drag.

'All right, go on.'

'I think time spent by an underwriter to make a decision is a good surrogate… you know… for the complexity of a case. Let's see logs for a decently-sized sample and let's have Rizwan study the data. I'm sure my assumption will be validated. We will find a significant chunk of applications which are a Yes and on which the underwriter spends close to no time. These are the cases we go after. What I'm saying is, the objective of the machine we make will be to find absolute-Yes cases in the 40 per cent lot, in the human underwriting lot, OK? And these, I'm sure, will be the overwhelming majority in that lot.'

'But what about the risk of wrong decisions?'

'Yeah, so, let's set an upper limit on the risk amount that the AI can take a decision on. Insurance amounts bigger than that will continue to go to underwriters. That reduces the risk. And in this way the most experienced underwriters will be valued even more. Machine and humans collaborate at first. After a few months, after we have proven that the cost of a few erroneous decisions by the learned machine is less than the money saved by working with a leaner underwriting department, we will start a transition towards full automation. By then the underwriting department will be weakened, too, so there will be little resistance.'

Mitesh nods slowly for a few seconds until what I've said settles deep in his mind and begins to excite him. He bums another cigarette from a colleague he spots in the smoking area. 'Now that's an action-oriented plan,' he states. 'That's a fucking plan, Saransh. We don't threaten the reinsurers. We optimize the risk. We increase the automation percentage. Bingo.'

'And… you will be able to fire about thirty to thirty-five people from the underwriting staff,' I say. 'As has been your heart's desire. Four to five will remain, though.'

'It's a compromise I'm willing to make,' Mitesh says with a smile.

'The only problem will be *Explainability*,' I say.

'Oh?'

'Machine decisions cannot be explained, remember? So, if the regulator asks us why we said Yes to a given case, and if that case is a machine-YES case, we won't be able to give them a legible reason.'

'We will factor that in the cost–benefit analysis,' Mitesh says. 'Worst case – it will cost a couple of lakhs in penalties.'

'Sounds good,' I say.

But it doesn't actually sound good. I've solved a considerable conceptual problem in a jiffy, but I feel neither pride nor exhilaration. The process through which the entire plan just came to me, all in one-piece, would have amazed me a month or so ago. But, as I pull smoke from the new cigarette that Mitesh has shared with me, it feels as if the cloud of guilt that I started the workday with has spread itself again all around me. What impulse drove me to solve the problem? What necessity? What fever?

To avoid these questions, I check my phone. There's a WhatsApp message from Jyoti. She has cooked something that she will bring with her in the evening. This tells me that she has recovered from her own gloominess. I ask her again about the Diwali week in Goa. 'Yes, let's do it!' she replies immediately.

'You remember about this Sunday, right?' Mitesh asks me.

I look up from my phone and hand back the cigarette to him. 'I thought you'd forgotten, given how drunk you were when you invited me.'

'No, no, how can I forget?'

'We are flying out to Goa on Monday, so it might be a bit hectic on Sunday.'

'Hey, come on, man. You said yes in Nashik. And Jyoti must come, too. What does she drink?'

'I think red wine will do. But don't bother. We will bring a bottle.'

'Then I will just make sure we don't fall short of it.' Mitesh drops the cigarette and squashes it with his shoe. 'You know,' he clears his throat before continuing, 'I'm a bit too emotionally attached to the implementation of new tech. I guess that's why it makes me angry when I see people… like Poonam today… putting up arbitrary roadblocks.'

'I don't think she said anything that we would not have found to be a roadblock ourselves.'

'I know, I know, but it's just her tone, yaar. What a negative bitch. Why couldn't she come up with what you offered now? She surely had more time than you. It's all attitude, man. I guess I'll have to tell Unni.'

'Maybe she's emotionally attached to the underwriting department. To the people she has worked with. Rizwan was suggesting something like that.'

'Hmm… Let's go?'

We leave the smoking area and walk back towards the main lobby. There, next to the turnstiles that give access to the elevators, I see a man wiping the leaves of a potted croton plant with a cloth. He's removing dust. That's his job. I wonder if a robot can do his job.

'You're right,' Mitesh says. 'It's obvious she is very attached to her old friends.'

'I must say I rate attachment with humans above attachment with tech,' I reply. It sounds more cutting than I wanted it to.

Mitesh looks at me with curiosity. 'And you?' he asks. 'What are you emotionally attached to?'

I think about it for a few seconds. I think of Jyoti. I think of my younger brother, who was born when I was eleven, and who is now studying computer engineering in Delhi. It makes me think of my parents in Muzaffarnagar – my mother watching a TV serial, my father having a secret drink in the storeroom, both content with the paths that their sons have charted in the bigger world. 'I don't know,' I say. 'Those who are close to me, I guess. Family.'

'That's true for everyone,' Mitesh says.

'What else can I say? I'm doing my job, man. There is no reason to be emotionally attached to this or that.'

I don't know about their effect on Mitesh, but my words strike me like a gong on a hollow vessel. We enter the lift. I think of the croton-cleaning man and try to probe my feelings. I do my job and he does his. Mine gives me a chance at intellectual satisfaction, his doesn't have that scope. But what play of intellect do I derive satisfaction from? The question overpowers me to an extent that when Mitesh asks me if I would like to present my approach on the underwriting project to Unnikrishnan next week, I find it impossible to even nod in response. I think of how iBlink was conceived by me, and how, now, it is I who will lay down the blueprint for the underwriting project as well. That's what I'm doing with my intellect, that's what my desire to exercise it is leading to. I'm making the SPG successful in cutting jobs. Rather, my intellect is making the SPG a monster that eats jobs. Or, my intellect's success is in eating jobs. Or, my intellect is the monster that eats jobs. I know that sometime next year the SPG will also initiate work on voice bots that utilize the phenomenal progress AI has made in processing and mimicking human voice. The bots will take over customer servicing; hundreds of telecallers will lose their jobs. And for my intellectual satisfaction I will help the SPG achieve that, too, in the best way possible.

The clink of the elevator reaching the sixth floor interferes with my train of thought. We walk across the lobby and head straight to Zepellin. At the room's entrance, affixed to the glass door, is the rectangular metallic plate bearing the room's name. My attention is drawn, for the nth time, to the error in the spelling. Once inside, I switch on my laptop and notice that Manpreet has sent me an email with the transfer policy attached. I open the document and start reading it, but I'm distracted. Somehow the spelling's wrongness is amplified for me today. It merges with all the niggles that the day has brought so far – the long car ride, Jyoti's messages, Poonam's presentation, Vijayalaxmi's phone call, my inputs on the underwriting project, my conflicting thoughts thereafter. Almost unthinkingly I pick up an A4 sized blank sheet among the many lying in front of me and, with a ballpoint pen, begin to draw some letters on it. After I draw them to my satisfaction, I shade them.

ZEPPELIN

'What are you doing?' George asks.

'I'm doing something for my intellectual satisfaction,' I say.

In a small drawer next to the TV there is a common stationery box. I walk up to it and pull out a roll of tape and a pair of scissors. Then I go outside the room and paste the A4 sheet with the correct spelling right over the metallic plate. The people inside can see me through the glass door. I take a couple of steps back to examine my handiwork. It is temporary, but it is correct. The next few seconds, in which nothing happens, feel simultaneously ridiculous and momentous.

When I enter the room again, I find Mitesh shaking his head and smiling. Poonam claps slowly, thrice. 'It takes a courageous man to confront life's toughest problems,' Ankita says, her words not irritating me this time.

TOPAZ

THE OLA CAB IS SMELLY IN THE FAMILIAR WAY OF CARS DRIVEN in endless shifts. Once on the highway, we roll down the windows. Jyoti is not conscious of it, but she is holding the fingers of my right hand in her left hand. 'This is so strange,' she says a few minutes into the ride. 'This going with you to your colleague's house. This Sunday lunch affair. His wife being there. The bourgeois prettiness of the thing, you know? It's just so strange to me.' She follows it up with something about October heat, how it makes the monsoons feel like a distant memory, how it's almost obscene that Mumbai has to deal with it after the deluge. I agree with her about the weather. Then we look out of our respective windows – at the huge hoardings selling apartments and shampoos and soap operas. Jyoti is still holding my fingers. Is she nervous? What did she mean by *strange*?

Forty minutes later we arrive at our destination in Wadala – a residential complex called Topaz. Four buildings, each with four floors. In that I find it similar to my Saibaba Complex, but then I see several expensive cars – two black

Audis, one red BMW, one white Mercedes – parked inside the complex. Such cars are not common in the society I live in.

Inside the B building, on the third floor, we press the bell outside Mitesh's flat. It is he who opens the door. 'I should have messaged you to not press the bell,' he says and hugs me perfunctorily.

His gaze lingers on Jyoti who is clad in a pair of tight gray jeans and an orange halter-neck top that leaves her shoulders bare. They smile, shake hands. I don't know how to interpret the hug Mitesh gave me (our first ever), but I'm glad he doesn't try it with Jyoti.

'Aryansh is sleeping,' Mitesh explains, pointing to a room on the far side of the lobby. 'And he's sensitive about the bell ringing. Always thinks it's a toy delivery from Flipkart or something and gets cranky when it isn't. Come in, come in.'

Jyoti hands Mitesh the bottle of wine we have brought. 'It's more for us, really,' she says with a wink. Mitesh laughs and puts the bottle in the crook of his arm. He is wearing a pair of baggy military-green shorts and a gray T-shirt that says *KRABI, Ao Nang Beach* above the image of a classic Volkswagen van swooshing on a road girded by palm trees. From his Thailand vacation last year, I conclude. 'Please, make yourselves comfortable,' he says, pointing towards the sofa in the living room. He then goes to the kitchen.

On the wall in front of us hangs a painting; it's an abstract piece, yet my imagination finds the form of a brown mountain in it. *How do you climb an abstract mountain?* I think, and for a moment I can't decide if the thought is silly or profound. Jyoti is looking out from the sliding window to our left – there is a football ground in sight, part of the sprawling luxury apartment complex situated across the road. Many sprinklers are at work there, creating jagged parabolas of water jets, several of which form a mini-rainbow at an angle.

Mitesh's wife, Priya, emerges from the kitchen. She is dressed in a loose-fitting Indian suit, the salwar white and the kurta bearing a pattern of tiny white flowers on a light-green fabric. There is a studied reserve in her manner and it makes me think of her as the kind of woman who would stay in the hotel room and fiddle with her worry beads while her husband prowled the beaches in Krabi. In the small talk that follows she claims that she has heard a lot about me. 'Mitesh says you're the engine of the Special Projects Group.' I allow myself to feel a bit flattered. She then talks about her job as a branch manager in a general insurance company, about how her company isn't focussing on technology and how that will turn out to be a mistake. 'They keep saying it's the future and they don't realize it's the present,' she says, her wide eyes carrying a fair bit of conviction . At her turn, Jyoti introduces herself as a 'journalist on a sabbatical.' The word journalist does something to Priya, who starts bemoaning the state of TV news channels in general and the miracle of prime-time shouting tournaments finding a gullible audience in particular. Jyoti then makes a point about print media being as bad. She calls the *Times* 'the shittiest of the shitty ones.' A blast of Sunday ads from the same paper is placed on the centre table between us, and so, feeling a pang of embarrassment on Priya's part, I start talking about the brown mountain I have seen in the painting. 'Mitesh's father drew this,' Priya tells us with a wry smile. 'He completed it just before he was diagnosed. I've never understood it.'

'Sometimes art is better not understood,' I say.

Priya smiles vacuously to my meaningless comment. From the room abutting the kitchen, Aryansh steps out rubbing his eyes. Priya introduces him to *uncle* and *aunty*, but Aryansh shows no interest in us and squirms out of his mother's hold. 'My time,' he shouts crankily, following which Priya switches on the large TV to our right. A cartoon show begins to play.

My mind travels back to thoughts of Alan Kurdi – same age as this child, wearing a similar red-and-blue combination that this child is dressed in. I give some sign of having made this connection – maybe a loud sniff, maybe a tiny shudder – for Jyoti places her hand on my left arm. Or maybe Jyoti does it just like that. I place my other hand on hers. These gestures, and perhaps the way we both end up looking at Aryansh, invite a misreading. 'So you guys getting married soon?' Priya asks us. All we can do in response is to withdraw immediately.

Mitesh emerges from the kitchen holding three glasses of wine. 'Priya doesn't like wine?' Jyoti asks. 'She stopped drinking after Aryansh was born,' Mitesh answers.

We clink glasses. After the first sip, I talk about the beautiful apartment complex on the other side of the road.

'The bonus this year, man…' Mitesh says, '…if all goes well then by April next year we should be able to sell this flat and buy a new one there.' So that's how that sentence ends, I think. I comment on the expensive cars in Topaz and in jest ask Mitesh if he's been hiding a Mercedes all this time. 'Oh, you bring up an interesting topic,' Priya says. Mitesh then tells a story about the owner of one of the BMWs, who when requested not to use the society's clean water to have his car washed, flat out refused. 'Things escalated quickly in our last society meeting. A car's need for clean water was hotly debated.'

'And not just that. One of the Audi owners complained that some children have scratched his car,' Priya adds. 'So now there are questions like whose children scratched whose car? Whose parents should pay which car-owner? That's why, you know, if we buy an expensive car it's better to be in a better residency. They have safe parking facilities there.'

Mitesh, Priya and I turn to look out the window. The water jets have stopped spitting.

'Is it teenagers?' Jyoti asks. 'The ones who scratch the cars.'

'No, no, these are children on tricycles,' Priya replies, 'Aryansh's age, or a little older. It's possible that they bump into parked cars and leave scratches. There isn't a lot of playing space here, na.'

'Big car people are really rotten,' Jyoti says. We all look towards her, bemused by the sweep of her comment.

'Well, they can be,' Priya adds with a shrug and a smile.

'I couldn't imagine – '

I'm interrupted by the sound of a steel plate falling in the kitchen. Mitesh grunts something under his breath as Priya rushes to check what has happened. This also distracts Aryansh from the cartoons. Apparently, some of the frozen kebabs are now on the floor. As Priya scolds the cook in Hindi, Aryansh tries to convey the scandal to the rest of us in the living room by clapping his hands once and making an oval with his lips. Jyoti finds the child's performance hilarious.

'It's become impossible to live without maids,' Mitesh says with a sigh, 'and it's impossible to get good maids in Mumbai.'

In the silence that follows Mitesh's comment I imagine the bais of Mumbai climbing up an abstract mountain. Jyoti tucks a lock of her hair behind her ear and turns the wine glass in her hand. She didn't like what Mitesh said.

'I think what is more troubling is middle-class Mumbaikars taking cheap domestic help for granted,' she says, taking a conspicuously smug sip from her glass.

'Yes, that's how it works,' says Mitesh, having missed Jyoti's point altogether. 'Priya works. I work. So we have a full-time ayah for Aryansh. Then there is the cleaner who comes twice a day. Then there is the cook who comes twice a day. They all want decent salaries, Diwali–Holi bonuses, whatnot. But the work they do is never good. Everything has to be explained to them. And always some mistake here, some mistake there. If nothing else, they just go on leave whenever they feel like it. The ayah, for example, hasn't come today.'

I try to react in a sympathetic manner. The shift from ridiculing a BMW owner to blaming Mumbai's bais strikes me as hypocritical, but also consistent with something else I am unable to name.

'Gadgets, modular kitchens, middle-class manners,' Jyoti says, 'these are alien to people you employ. And anyone can make an error like dropping a plate in the kitchen. How much do you pay them?' From Jyoti's tone I know that she is preparing to launch into an argument. It makes me nervous.

Mitesh fidgets. 'We pay them well. Between the three of them they get about 35,000 rupees each month.'

'Are they related to each other? Part of the same family?' Jyoti asks.

'No.'

'Then why are you saying *they* get 35,000? Thirty-five thousand is your outgoing. They don't look at it that way, right? You know what I mean?'

'All right, all right,' Mitesh concedes, shuffling in his seat.

'Yeah. They are three different people running three different households. Who has the lowest salary among the three?'

'The cook,' Mitesh answers while looking at me quizzically. 'The cook gets 6,000.'

Priya comes out of the kitchen muttering something I can't hear. She is carrying a tray with some snacks for us, and a bowl that has something for Aryansh, who is back to being hypnotized by the cartoons and almost drops the bowl to the floor when Priya tries to hand it to him. 'I've asked

Meenu to wash the kebabs,' Priya says while taking her place next to Mitesh, who shakes his head in disappointment.

'So, 6,000,' Jyoti continues, taking a swig from her glass. 'Given that it is impossible to live in Mumbai without household staff, I'm sure your cook has employed a cook herself at a much lower price. And so on it goes.'

This makes me laugh.

'She works in some other places, too.' It is Priya who answers this time, and I consider it noteworthy that she was listening in on our conversation while berating the bai.

'How many other places?' asks Jyoti, and when there is no answer for a few seconds, adds, 'maybe she's too hassled, too busy.'

'Yeah, possible,' Priya says.

'What's your point, Jyoti?' Mitesh asks with a wave of his hand as if removing some abstract clutter to get to the point. 'That we are paying her too little?'

'Yes, everyone in India pays their household staff insufficiently. Rather, everyone gets them too cheaply.'

Mitesh shrugs. Priya gives a part-dismissive, part-placating smile. I don't know what to do, so I smell my wine.

'If I'm paying for a service, I have the right to point out when the service is not good,' Mitesh makes his point.

'That's one way to look at things,' Jyoti says.

'And there are other ways to look at it?'

'Yes! You are not entitled to anything. You are able to avail the service because the ones who provide it have limited options. They work at these wages because society wants to keep it that way.'

'Society? How so?' Mitesh asks.

'Structural stuff,' Jyoti answers. 'The caste system, of course. And other things. Basically, your staff can make an error, man… what's the big deal? You are anyway ripping them off.'

'The caste system?' Mitesh's face is a diagram of confusion. 'That's one of the most cognitively dissonant things I have heard in a while.'

'Cognitively dissonant? Really? Well, it isn't. I will answer, but first I'll take a refill.' Jyoti gets up from the sofa and goes to the kitchen to fill her glass.

Mitesh looks at me with twisted lips. I feel hot in my ears. In the kitchen Jyoti starts a conversation with the cook, while outside, in the living room, there is silence except for the chirp of the cartoons and the whirr of the air conditioner.

When Jyoti returns it is I who speak first: 'Can we talk about something else? Something less controversial than the work ethic of bais and the complex relationship of their purchasing power with the cost of living in Mumbai? And the infinitely recursive loop in which each household needs household staff. Can we?'

'Mitesh,' Jyoti ignores me, 'hope you don't mind. Because I'm someone who says whatever's on her mind.'

'Oh, no problem. I enjoy a good chat, always.'

'I sense a level of sahab-ness in you and I can't resist.'

'The caste system. You said something about it,' Mitesh says. He has taken the bait. I feel like facepalming.

'Oh yes. I was. It's a system of oppression, right? And so old that it has reached our DNA or some other equivalent part of our essence. I don't know, I'm not a science person. Not even a social science person. But the system ends up creating hierarchies of subjugation... entire populations who accept less. And that's what feeds our lifestyles – yours, mine, Saransh's – basically the whole middle class. I find it obscene when one of us complains.'

Not a very sharp critique – that's my immediate thought.

Mitesh begins to respond, 'These are all good things to speak about, Jyoti, but – '

' – and, by the way, your cook works in six houses,' Jyoti interrupts him, her voice making no attempt to conceal her excitement. 'Six. She comes from Dombivali. She is on her feet from 5 a.m. to 9 p.m., every single day. It doesn't take much to know.'

'Oh come on, Jyoti,' Mitesh groans. 'Are *we* oppressing someone? Are *we* responsible for caste or any such thing? Priya and I didn't even know our caste until we got married. Aryansh may never get to know and we like it that way. We don't know the caste of any of our maids. We don't ask for it before we employ them. I know of people who wouldn't let a person from a lower caste enter their kitchen. We are not those people. We just pay the market rate and demand quality – what's wrong with that?'

'Several things,' Jyoti speaks softly now as if we have arrived at the crux of the matter, 'but the biggest thing wrong with that is perhaps the failure to think about what keeps the poor poor in this country. Also, the failure to see oneself as a contributor to that process. An indirect contributor, sure. If that makes you feel good.'

Contrition, guilt, that's where she's getting at again. We sit in an air-conditioned room and talk about the poor, while the only poor person in the house works in the kitchen, unable to understand what is being argued in the language of her masters. But can guilt be a general prescription for a condition of privilege? Should everyone on the right side of the system feel guilty about being there? And then do what? I understand that Jyoti only wants the entitled ones to be aware of how the system is inclined to their benefit. But is awareness enough?

'The poor are not poor because of us,' Mitesh declares. 'The poor are poor because of themselves.'

'Really?' Jyoti obviously doesn't like that. I don't like that either.

'Yes! I will give you an example,' Mitesh says.

'I just told you how hard your cook works,' Jyoti says. 'Wow, man, that's a really nasty thing to say. Really inconsiderate.'

Priya, looking annoyed, rises from the sofa and goes to the kitchen. We hear her giving the cook stern instructions about the raita.

'It's true. What I said is very true,' says Mitesh. 'Our ayah's son is a drunkard. She worked hard and gave him decent schooling, even made him attend college. But he doesn't contribute to the household now. Just drinks and drinks. And tortures his mother for money. And when he doesn't drink, he lazes around. She complains about him a lot.'

'Couldn't his laziness or drinking habit,' I step in, 'whatever it is… I mean… couldn't it be seen as less a cause of poverty and more an effect of it?'

Mitesh is a bit surprised to hear from me. 'I knew someone would say that,' he says. *But not you*, he doesn't need to add that. The index finger on his right hand, the hand clasping the wine glass, is raised to the ceiling at an odd angle. He continues: 'Tell me one thing. Shouldn't the poor take some responsibility for getting out of poverty? It is obvious that they have to work harder.'

'But isn't your cook already working harder than anyone in this room?' says Jyoti.

'Her working hard is the *effect* of someone else in her family not working hard,' Mitesh says, looking towards me with a triumphant expression. 'Women usually have to bear the burden of stupid men,' he adds.

'That's the one smart thing you've said in all this time,' Jyoti says.

'Oh, come on, Jyoti,' Priya joins us in the living room. 'Haven't you heard stories of how slum dwellers refuse to move to flats offered to them?'

'See, my theory is...' Mitesh interjects, 'my theory is that anyone who moves with the times will not be poor.'

'So you're saying that the millions and millions of poor people in India are poor because they've refused to move with the times? Because they have refused to adapt?' Jyoti asks.

'Refused to adapt. Failed to adapt. Whatever you journalist types want to call it. But that's the truth.'

'I am wondering how many stories of resilience and kindness – resilience and kindness in the face of extreme poverty – will I need to tell you from my experience as a journalist before you budge an inch from your stupid views.'

Mitesh sniggers. 'Resilience, kindness, et cetera, these are irrelevant to this debate,' he says. 'We are talking economics here.'

'Oh, are we?' Jyoti says with faux surprise, followed by a shake of her head.

The argument continues. Priya brings back attention to her point about slum dwellers. Mitesh utters one inconsiderate thing after another, his embattled attitude clearly showing itself as germinating from a horrible conviction – that the poor desire poverty. I think of his vulgarity again, and relate it to another vulgarity that I've known intimately. In Muzaffarnagar, my father often said the ghastliest things about Muslims. These were things that affected my attitude towards Muslim mates at school, things that I believed in until I got out of that small town and saw the bigger world. But now, hearing Mitesh and Priya argue with Jyoti, I realize that the world that I have reached, the world that made me discard my father's notions as delusions of hate, is also a world where someone like Mitesh, who in all probability saw neither scarcity nor disadvantage, could acquire the vulgarity that he now brandishes unknowingly. He had all the exposure that I, working hard to get out of Muzaffarnagar, did not. But perhaps exposure is only material to be reflected upon – it still requires a self that can reflect. I credit myself then, as a man of some substance, as a man whose journey has value, as a man who sees and considers. This realization grants me a sense of serenity such that I want the increasingly bitter (though still theatrically polite) argument running around me to stop. I get up from the sofa and approach Aryansh. I say 'Hello' to him twice and try to shake his hand. It's an offer he ignores. I ruffle his hair, which angers him enough to slap my hand away. An idea comes to my mind then, an idea that I think will distract everyone.

'Guys, do you know that Jyoti is working on a children's book?' I say.

Suddenly interrupted, the three of them turn silent. I repeat what I have said. Jyoti looks at me with scrunched eyebrows. Mitesh smirks.

'Really?' Priya asks. 'Like *Harry Potter*?'

'No, no,' I say, 'for an age group slightly younger than that. Am I right, Jyoti?'

'Yes,' affirms Jyoti, her lips immediately pursed after that one word.

'I would have believed it more if you'd said that Jyoti is writing a non-fiction book about how the middle-class is sucking the country dry,' says Mitesh.

The sarcasm in Mitesh's comment is thankfully ignored by Jyoti. Also by Priya, who seems genuinely interested. 'I keep looking for good picture books for Aryansh,' she says. 'It's so important to inculcate the habit early on. Already he spends so much time on TV. What's your book about, Jyoti?'

Jyoti is reluctant to answer. She looks at me, then takes a deep breath. 'It's about a girl named Shazia and her younger brother Azlan. They have to survive an entire night in their house because their parents are stuck outside the city.'

'Oh, so are there nasty villains in the story? Like in *Home Alone*?' Priya asks.

'No, but there is a curfew-like situation in the city. And there are shadows – called *The Forces* – that haunt the house that night,' Jyoti answers. 'The Forces claim that they own the house. They call the family *The Others*.'

'Wow, so interesting,' Priya says. 'Is this complete? Is it going to be out soon?'

'I'm still writing it.'

'How long does it take to finish a book like this?' Mitesh asks, narrowing his eyes, perhaps to make it a *genuine* question.

'I don't know. I'm writing one for the first time, you see. I think it's more than a year now that I've been trying.'

'Wow,' Priya says. 'I see it takes a lot of effort to write even a children's book.'

I know Priya didn't mean to be snarky, but with the reek of the earlier argument still lingering, I realize no chances should be taken. 'Actually, writers can hit a mini-crisis sometimes,' I say.

'Why do you have to bring this up here, Saransh?' Jyoti asks angrily. Shocked by her reaction, I can only open and close my mouth once.

'What sort of mini-crises?' Mitesh asks.

Jyoti takes a moment to compose herself. 'The news,' she says. 'The news cycle. All the news from all over the world. Of all the violence that people have to face, that children have to face. The relentless violence. It makes things a bit too clear, I would say, like how threats are more real than mere shadows. Take Syria, for example. Bombs fall from the sky and they smash everything. Children like Shazia and Azlan are blown to bits. There is no surviving the night in that sense. The Forces always win. The story, if there ever were a story, terminates with a bloody bang.'

It takes a few seconds for Mitesh and Priya to misunderstand what Jyoti has just said. 'But you aren't writing the book for Syrian kids, are you?' Mitesh asks. 'Are Shazia and Azlan Syrian?'

'No they aren't,' Jyoti answers. 'They aren't from anywhere. Though they could be from anywhere. From Kashmir, say. Or Gaza.'

'See but that's not the point, Mitesh,' I say, stepping in. 'The thing to understand is how do you write such a book in a world where children face horrible things. That's probably where Jyoti is coming from.'

'Thanks for explaining my situation, Saransh,' Jyoti says acidly.

'Oh, in that case, she just has to stop thinking about these things,' Mitesh advises with fake casualness in his voice. He then leans back on the sofa – to him, the problem is solved.

'That's a great suggestion. So, tell me, how does one stop thinking about these things?' Jyoti asks, the shift in her tone betraying some anguish.

Sensing this as weakness, Mitesh grins impudently and repeats, 'How does one stop thinking about these things? Well, stop noticing them.'

Jyoti vents air through her lips making a sound of pure exasperation. The mocking lilt in Mitesh's voice is offensive to me, too – its span of ridicule covers not only Jyoti but also that dead child with his face buried in wet sand. I feel compelled to say something to shatter Mitesh's comfort. 'Children like Aryansh have been dying in Syria, Mitesh,' I say, 'so I guess *you* should be thinking about these things, too. Imagine Aryansh being blown up by a bomb.'

Almost instantly the room's atmosphere alters to something that can have no pretence of mirth in it. Priya walks up to Aryansh, takes the near-empty bowl from the child's hands and proceeds to keep it in the kitchen. Mitesh, not grinning anymore, scratches the back of his head and then signals to me to step outside for a smoke. I look towards Jyoti, who is looking down to the floor and pinching her eyelids. I am sure she's angry with me, too. 'Lunch is ready,' Priya speaks from the kitchen. Jyoti stands up and walks towards the kitchen to help. Mitesh and I leave the flat and climb down a flight of stairs to a landing between floors. There, we light cigarettes next to a window that we will use to expel the smoke. The first drag is deep, silent – solid ground after quicksand.

'Your girlfriend is too sensitive,' Mitesh says at the third drag, 'and about far too many things.'

'And you are insensitive,' I say. 'About far too many things.'

'You know... don't take it personally... but I have a theory that a lot of people act extra sensitive to distract themselves from their own failures in life.'

'There could be an opposite theory as well. A lot of people who think they are successful are actually just insensitive pricks.'

Mitesh looks out of the window, turning thoughtful. That he hasn't taken any offence at what I said disappoints me somewhat.

'I work honestly,' he says with a sigh. 'I have a family. That much is enough. Who has the time for the rest? The world has hazaar problems. Once you have a family you will see how all idealism goes for a toss.'

'I don't believe you've ever been much of an idealist, Mitesh. You're a practical man. Always have been, I'm sure. And that's fine. Then be practical, no? Don't offer opinions about things you don't even think about.'

'You're very influenced by her.'

'Maybe.'

I move my arm past him and quash my cigarette stub on the face of the wall outside the window. Mitesh then does the same with his stub. There are beads of sweat above his upper lip.

'You told me once that she doesn't like the work that we are doing in SPG,' he asks me.

'Yeah.'

'Guess that's something that I can talk to her about? Considering I've *thought* about it enough.'

'You want to make this lunch more difficult?'

'I just want to know what she thinks about it. Surely, she has thought about it, too. With you.'

We go up the stairs and walk into the living room. Mitesh speaks to Aryansh loudly and crouches down to the child's level, asking him questions about the cartoons that he is watching. Jyoti and Priya are standing next to the dining table right outside the kitchen, their demeanour with each other more convivial than I expected it to be. The food looks plentiful and, hoping that the scene has normalized, I allow myself to feel hungry.

'I heard that you don't think very highly of our work, Jyoti,' Mitesh says.

'Whoever gave you that idea,' Jyoti says, throwing a sharp glance at me. I spread my arms briefly, helplessly.

'I heard you have some ethical concerns regarding it,' Mitesh continues.

'Kebabs, butter chicken, rice, rotis, salad, raita,' Priya says. 'Let's start with the kebabs.'

'I don't have any issues with it, actually,' Jyoti says. 'Is there any more alcohol?'

'No issues with it?'

'Is there more wine? No problem if there isn't. But lovely if there is.'

'Yes, yes, there is wine,' Mitesh says and picks up Jyoti's glass for a refill. Priya, Jyoti and I sit at the dining table. Mitesh returns with the glass full and, taking his place next to Priya, says, 'Guess we don't want to talk about it.' No one responds.

'The kebabs are good,' he adds after having a couple of pieces. 'Priya, give some to Meenu, too. She's worked hard.' After saying this he looks at Jyoti as if he's done something that merits commenting upon. I feel incensed, and from the hard look on Jyoti's face I know that she feels the same. Priya gets up and hands a plate with a couple of kebab pieces and some chutney to Meenu, the cook, who is sitting on the kitchen floor.

'She can sit here,' Jyoti says, pointing to an empty chair at the dining table.

'Huh?' Priya reacts, then shoots a glance towards Mitesh.

'I think she's happy there,' clarifies Mitesh.

Jyoti leaves the dining table and proceeds to sit next to Meenu.

'Jyoti, please don't make a scene,' Priya urges.

Jyoti ignores Priya and looks at Mitesh. 'I'm beginning to think that in your case, Mitesh sahab,' she pauses to take a bite of her kebab and a sip of her wine, 'the problems I have with your work are nothing compared to the problems I have with you, with the kind of person that you are.' She then looks towards Meenu and winks.

In the next fifteen seconds, Meenu wolfs down her kebab, dumps her plate in the sink, and runs outside the flat.

The moment Meenu is outside, Mitesh bangs his spoon down on his plate. 'This is too much, Saransh,' he complains to me. All his smug satisfaction from a couple of minutes ago has turned sour.

'I think Jyoti and I should leave,' I say in a low voice.

'I think so, too,' Mitesh says, his mouth rigid, the sweat above his upper lip threatening to trickle over.

We do not wait for the elevator and take the stairs instead. As we climb down, Jyoti releases an elongated 'fuck' from under her breath. Outside the building, as we walk past the expensive cars in the parking lot, she says, 'Do you fucking tell him our sex positions, too.'

'...'

'You clearly have no regard for what I may and may not want to share.'

'I'm sorry.'

'This is so not done, Saransh.'

'Yeah, I'm sorry.'

'And, seriously, how does he know what I think about your work?'

'I told him that after our first meeting. To tell him that there are people like you who think we're doing something bad.'

'Oh, so you told him because you wanted *him* to have doubts?' Jyoti says. 'What an idea!'

'Yeah, bad idea.'

'Anyway, let's scratch a car now,' she says, pointing at a parked Mercedes.

This makes me laugh, albeit only nervously, for it takes me a moment to strike out the possibility that she meant it.

Jyoti repeats the elongated 'fuck'. 'Your workmate is a serious jerk, man,' she says. 'Standard variety, though. The kind they produce in bulk these days. I'm sure he thinks he's a family man and all that.'

'Yes.'

'What a bastard. And his wife has no opinions of her own, I tell you.'

Waiting for our cab outside Topaz, I take Jyoti's hand in mine. 'I should not have raised your difficulties with writing the book, especially not with someone like Mitesh,' I say.

'Hmm… but I must say, you are quite a decent man in comparison,' she says. Then she interlaces her fingers with mine and lifts this combined entity to her lips.

The gesture surprises me, so much so that in the very next second, I am struck by the realization that I'm in love with Jyoti.

'Hilarious how he banged his spoon,' says Jyoti with a chuckle.

'Your sitting next to Meenu really riled him up.'

'For Mitesh, all that is wrong in the world is happening to others, elsewhere. How convenient is that?' she says.

'To Mitesh, that's somehow to his credit.'

Our cab arrives. 'Thank god we left that place early,' Jyoti says. 'How can you work with him?'

'I don't have to enquire about his worldview at the office,' I say while entering the cab.

'His worldview is clear,' says Jyoti. 'And there's no changing it. It is yours that needs to settle this way or that.'

The destination we have punched for the cab is of a restaurant close to my place. A few minutes into the ride, my phone rings. I fear it is Mitesh, ready to give me an earful about all that happened at lunch. But it's not him. It's

Vijayalaxmi. I haven't talked to her after receiving the email from Manpreet. I don't take the call.

'Who was that? Mitesh?' Jyoti asks.

'Someone called Vijayalaxmi. She's a LOE I met in Hyderabad. She's been asking me for a transfer to Mumbai.'

'LOEs are the people you guys are going to fire, right?'

'Yes.'

Jyoti turns to look outside her window, then says, 'Maybe you should just tell her the truth.'

I rerun in my mind the moment from a little while ago when Jyoti kissed my fingers and called me a decent man. It makes me feel heady, happy. It's not the wine, it's love. A *decent man in comparison*. I feel a sudden urge to remove the last two words from that assessment, an urge to do something decent in the absolute. Or perhaps an urge to harm the man whose house we stormed out of because we couldn't make peace with his indecency. I dial back Vijayalaxmi's number.

'Hello, Vijayalaxmi, this is Saransh.'

'Yes, sir. I call you, sir.'

'I want to tell you something, Vijayalaxmi. I want to tell you that… instead of looking for a transfer, you should start looking for a new job in a new company.'

'Why, sir? Why new job?'

'Because BLIC is going to ask all the LOEs to leave. In April next year. The LOE role is going to be finished. You understand?'

'Meaning there will be no LOE in branch after six months?'

'Yes.'

'Why, sir?'

'Because BLIC does not need LOEs anymore.'

She is silent for a few seconds. Then, 'OK, sir.'

'I'm sorry, Vijayalaxmi.'

'OK, sir. Thank you for help, sir.' She disconnects the call.

Jyoti is looking at me with wide eyes. 'Wow,' she whispers, 'you told her.'

I guess the smile I am wearing is a proud smile.

'What now?' Jyoti asks.

'I don't know,' I say. I can't help giggling a bit.

'You told her the truth, wow.'

'Yes, I did.'

'That's amazing.'

'I guess it is.'

'My god… that's just made me a bit horny,' she says and kisses me on the lips.

REBELLIONS

MORJIM, NORTH GOA. WE HAVE RENTED THE SECOND FLOOR of a private villa right next to the beach. From the outside there is nothing villa-like about the place – a cynical person could see it as three cuboids painted yellow and white and stacked atop each other. But the interiors are tastefully done, with the decor and the furniture managing to convey some sort of concordance with slow coastal life. To me, nothing signifies it more than the large framed picture in the living room. Captioned *The Sea Staring At Tourists*, it shows precisely what (according to me) the text suggests – a wide shot including tourists of various complexions and all the different paces of sea-side enjoyment. Jyoti doesn't like the caption. 'So horribly inaccurate,' she says. 'The photo is perfect, yes, but this perfection also tells the viewer that there is someone behind that camera. So how is it the sea staring at anything? I'm being too literal, true, but still. Like, isn't it just impossible to frame a photograph of the sea staring at tourists? I mean, the sea should be able to *see* the entire beach, no? Why are we restricted to what we are looking at? And also, what we call the sea is only bits of the surface of the sea, isn't it?'

She is right, though in a useless way. I'm beginning to adore that about her. Anyway, what both of us prefer over the photograph is the sea view from the balcony attached to our bedroom. This morning, our first here, I wake up to the sight of her leaning on the balcony railing, her hands holding a cup of coffee, her lips moving as if to a song. I stand up, parting the sliding door to the balcony and walk up to her. She looks at me and smiles, her face made mellow by the morning light and whatever it was that she was murmuring. I pull her cup to my lips and take a sip. 'So, do we agree on *special* now?' I ask. This is a reminder of a little tiff we had just before booking this accommodation. She'd wanted Goa to be a budget trip; I'd wanted it to be special. We had argued about the word *special* with Jyoti impressing upon me how there is no thesaurus in the whole world in which I would find the words *special* and *expensive* as synonyms. On the balcony, though, Jyoti gives a fake sigh and says, 'I guess you won.'

The expensive part of this special vacation is being covered by me. Jyoti is paying for drinks and daily scooter rentals, all of which will amount to about 10 per cent of our overall expense. I don't mind that, of course. I am, in fact, more concerned about whether even this 10 per cent is a burden for her. Each time she spends her money my curiosity about its source is kindled. By my estimate she's been unemployed for more than six months now, which, given the living expenses in Mumbai, can make a serious dent in anyone's savings. I don't know what her plans are. There is some confidence in Jyoti – or perhaps it is carelessness – that I do not comprehend. It may even be that I feel envious of it. The day before we went to Mitesh's house, I'd gotten in touch with a friend in publishing and learned some things about the industry's economics. I was told that even if a major publisher were to take Jyoti's book there was no way that the advance could exceed a lakh or thereabouts. It was clear that as a project, which Jyoti had often mentioned as the reason for putting other things on hold, the children's book was not going to lead to much in the way of earnings. Later that day when I told her this, she just shrugged. Jyoti is not frivolous about spending her money. But she can show such casualness towards earning it that it makes no sense. My own case is the complete reverse, and I wonder if this points to a more fundamental difference between us.

On our first night in Goa, after a couple of glasses of the cheap red wine that Jyoti bought earlier in the day, I broach the topic of her journalism career. 'I don't know anything about what really happened in your last job,' I say. We are on the bed and the sliding door to the balcony is open. Jyoti is plucking her eyebrows, peering into the compact mirror lodged between her knees. 'So, tell me, why did you quit?' I ask.

Jyoti responds with silence at first, a silence in which I note how, sound-wise, a sea is blandly repetitive. Then, 'I didn't quit, I was asked to leave.'

'Really? Why?'

'I got myself into trouble.'

'What kind of trouble?'

'I can't tell you the specifics, Saransh. I was investigating something fishy in a government engineering college in Rajasthan. Sand… being stolen from the playground… for a private construction site.'

'And?'

'And I was staying in the boys' hostel.'

'Why were you staying there?'

'Because the boys had been complaining to their alumni network about their playground access being cut. Because the boys' hostel was the closest to the playground. Because I thought staying inside the campus would be better. Because the boys were allies, so to speak.'

'OK, so what happened next?'

'The college authorities found out. They threatened the boys with disciplinary action.'

'And then?'

'And then the dean complained to my magazine. About how I had taken residence in the boys' hostel. About how I was degrading the morals of underage boys. His complaint all but specified that I was having sex with the boys. They had some of the boys allege all sorts of things, of course.'

'How did your magazine react?'

'The Chief Editor asked me to return. He said he couldn't allow me to pursue the story any further.'

'And you did? Go back, I mean.'

'Yes. I came back to Mumbai. He was very angry with me, my boss. I told him I had enough material to publish a story. I told him that the college authorities were just trying to intimidate us. I told him that the allegations against me won't have any currency once the story was out.'

'What did he say?'

'He told me that the students were in the way of danger because of me.'

'So, then?'

'I was angry. Very angry. At that time I didn't really believe that any harm could come to the students. I thought that was a bluff. I was not thinking straight, I guess. So that evening, I wrote a series of tweets about the story.'

'Oh-kay.'

'A few hours after I posted my tweets, I got an email from the Chief Editor demanding for them to be deleted. I was in the rebellious mode so I decided to ignore it. I did delete the tweets the next morning. But then, in the office that day, I was handed my termination letter. They gave me a cheque with three months' salary as severance. I remember thinking *that's not a bad deal.*'

I try to find a strain of anger, or anguish, in Jyoti's voice. There is none. There is something else – a sense of being beyond bother. I shift sideways to look at her better. She is done with the eyebrows. Now she is examining her face in the mirror, stretching different parts of her skin with her fingers. Her lips are pouted in concentration. The matter-of-factness in all this – her telling an all-important story while paying attention to something banal – perturbs me. Running parallel to this perturbation is an inchoate fantasy of domesticity, of the continuation of this companionship, on a soft bed, in a soft house, in a soft life, where all the world's edges are blunted. I place my hand on her bare thigh and caress it.

'So, what happened next?' I ask.

'I broke up with him. The Chief Editor.'

'What!?'

'Yes.'

'Oh, OK.'

'I had a lot of time after that, of course. I downloaded dating apps, joined book clubs, joined a dance class… things like that. I did look for a new job. But thanks to my ex-boss, also my ex, I became a bit infamous. I was the stubborn girl who had tweeted against her employer. I was the girl with a dubious character. People didn't really want to hire me. They would never say these were the reasons, of course. I could have looked for something outside India, at least I like imagining it was possible, but I didn't want to. I started freelancing. But young freelancers like me don't get their expenses paid. So I limited myself to covering cultural shit in Bombay, which was stupid work for someone with my experience. I still do it sometimes, but the online-only places that show interest don't pay very well. The severance money will run out soon, so my plan is to combine freelancing with free-riding.'

'Free-riding?'

'Yeah. On my father's money,' Jyoti says. I look on, confused. She shuts the mirror and places it on the bedside table next to her. This is the first time she's mentioned her father or his money to me. 'My father is a super famous corporate lawyer, Saransh,' she says. 'Has a house in South Bombay. I'm a South Bombay girl, you see, daughter of a rich man, everything on my beck and call… all of that shit. And I think my father will love having me depend on him for a while. Though I must say free-riding on your money is much better.' She waves her arm in a semicircle to refer to the luxuries of the room – its four-poster bed, its antique ceiling fan, its lavishly upholstered furniture.

'My pleasure,' I say.

I know she's said the last bit in jest. But the part about her father has made me think. That's the cushion she has. That's what allows her to be careless. I can't help but feel a pang of envy. My father, a clerk in the irrigation department of the UP government, will retire next year with a meagre corpus and an even more modest pension.

In the morning the property manager informs us that a buffet breakfast has been arranged on the long sea-side verandah on the ground floor. We arrive for breakfast hand in hand, like a couple on a honeymoon, which we practically are. A big family of ten people from three generations – they've taken the first two floors – eat raucously at a large table.

Their volume lowers only slightly after our arrival. We load our plates with scrambled eggs, toast and two kinds of sausage, and seat ourselves on the table farthest from the family. I look at my phone a couple of times while we are eating, something which Jyoti sneers at. I'm expecting some iBlink updates from Rizwan.

After we are done eating, Jyoti walks up to get us some coffee. She requests one of the stewards to wrap some sandwiches in foil; we are going to the beach after breakfast. I notice how she's both easy-going and firm with the steward. This, and other things – her high bun, her unpierced ears, her flip-flops, her white summer dress – begin to convey a practical casualness that I now attribute to the financial security she's always had. A rich girl, I remind myself.

'So excited about going to the beach,' Jyoti says on returning to the table, showing off the packed sandwiches in her hand.

'Me too,' I respond.

'Ideally, we should have been there before breakfast.'

My phone beeps once with a notification.

It is a WhatsApp message typed in a South-Indian language I cannot identify. Only my name, appended with *Sir,* is typed in English. The more notable thing is that it appears inside a group named *BLIC LOEs TOGETHER!!*

'What happened?' Jyoti asks me. Perhaps my face shows my surprise to some degree.

'Wait,' I say. I copy the message and paste it in Google translate on my phone. The sender seems to be sincerely requesting me to share more information about *the conspiracy of Mumbai people*.

'Everything all right, Saransh?' Jyoti asks again. 'Are we going to the beach or not?'

'Vijayalaxmi leaked the info,' I say.

'What?' Jyoti doesn't comprehend at first. Then her eyes widen and a smile begins to form on her face. 'She told others?' she asks.

'It looks like that.' I hand the phone to her.

'Oh my God,' says Jyoti. She puts the phone on the table and claps in glee. 'This is awesome. But it shows you've left the group. Why did you leave the group?'

'Fuck, Jyoti, what else could I do?' I say.

'Answer the questions they're asking,' Jyoti says in a tone that suggests that answering the questions is the most natural course of action.

'Let's go to the beach,' I say.

'Screw the beach,' Jyoti says. 'Saransh, answer them. Tell them how it is all going to happen. Tell them everything. Tell them about the interviews.'

'Really?'

'Yes,' Jyoti says. 'This is the chance, Saransh. This is the chance to change things.'

'Let's go to the beach. I'll think about it.'

Jyoti protests by first raising and then dropping her arms. I pick up my phone and look at WhatsApp. They have added me to the group again. 'Saransh sir, please be part of this group,' someone named Chaitanya has typed in. I check and find that, including me, there are only thirteen members in the group right now. This brings some relief – as of now the leak is localized. Vijayalaxmi is in the group.

But she's not an admin, so it was probably not her decision to form this group. I notice that Chandrasekhar and Raja – the two other LOEs from Hyderabad-1 – are playing the admin role. It seems that only four to five branches know about it till now – branches that the Hyderabad-1 LOEs are close to, I surmise.

'What's happening?' asks Jyoti.

'They've added me to the group again.'

'Don't mean to be alarmist, Saransh, but you know this can't be stopped now, right?'

'The news hasn't spread a lot.'

'It will, Saransh. When something is leaked it spreads. Leak equals spread. No leak contains itself.'

I exhale, put my phone face-down on the table, and hold my head in my hands. Jyoti touches my forehead and pushes it up. 'What are you worried about?' she asks.

'I'm the one behind this leak, Jyoti. I should not have told Vijayalaxmi.'

'You told Vijayalaxmi because you didn't want to give her false hope.'

'I told Vijayalaxmi because I was irritated with Mitesh.'

'Are you sure that's the reason?' asks Jyoti.

I can't answer. There are too many reasons why I told Vijayalaxmi what I did. One of them is that I love Jyoti and want her to love me. Or perhaps that's the only reason. Do we ever really know our reasons?

'Saransh, you did what you did because it felt right,' says Jyoti. 'You were happy after telling her, I remember. And now Vijayalaxmi has done what feels right to her. There is no way to run away from this now.'

My anxiety forces me to pick up my phone again. There is a message from Poonam.

Unni talked to me. Said I'm an important member of the team blah blah... that Mitesh can get excited sometimes. What's happening? Did you or Mitesh say anything to him?

'What?' Jyoti asks.

'Nothing.'

'Let's go to the beach then.'

I turn my phone silent. We climb down a staircase in one corner of the verandah and walk towards the beach. Just then a bright sun emerges from behind the clouds and the sand and the sea in front of us begin to glitter. I spread beach towels on one of the three canopy beds set up by the property owners. We are about twenty metres away from the water.

Jyoti removes her dress to reveal a black bikini. 'You coming?' she asks me.

'I'll be here for a bit,' I say.

'OK.' She kisses me on the cheek and runs off towards the sea.

I lie down and close my eyes; the sun stings my skin. I try to savour the burst of red under my eyelids, but there is too much going on inside my head, too many scenarios playing themselves out. Rizwan's machine is learning and what that machine is going to do is irreversible. But if all the LOEs come to know of it, and if all of them decide to raise hell about it, there is a chance that the company will reconsider. But do I want the company to reconsider? Isn't there a part of me that wants to protect the project, to minimize the damage, to inform Mitesh and Unnikrishnan right away about what I have set in motion?

I realize that I have placed myself in a situation in which, whether I choose to act this way or that, there will be unpleasant – to say the least – consequences.

I open my eyes. A blazing whiteness bursts through the red. I want to avoid looking at my phone, so I decide to enter the water. I stand up at once and take off my T-shirt and bermudas. 'Hey, watch me,' Jyoti shouts from the water. A big wave is forming behind her. She's positioning herself to jump in its direction, hoping to be carried with it. The wave arrives, Jyoti jumps, I watch. Jyoti is invisible for the next three or four seconds only to emerge very close to me, right at the shore. 'Oh god, oh god, oh my god, that was amazing,' she exclaims. Her performance makes me laugh. I run towards the water, towards Jyoti, in a clownish way, and jump in.

Fifteen minutes later we come out of the water and lie belly-down on the canopy bed. A sheer white cloth is draped over the top and the sides of the bed. A little wind is now blowing on it, just as it would if this were an advertisement for Goa. 'Ah, this feels good,' says Jyoti.

This feels good, yes. But I am connecting the feeling with something else, too. I am thinking – this is where I am. This is where I have reached. This is where I have reached from Muzaffarnagar. This hotel, this beach, this beach bed, this sun. I am thinking about my parents who have never had a vacation like this. I am thinking about growing up in a small city where even the idea of a woman in a bikini could cause a riot. I am thinking about how I reached here, about how I did everything I could do to reach here. To reach here I've ticked all the boxes that needed to be ticked. And this ticking of boxes is the only measure of right and wrong I've known. My value as a person has always been tied to how flawlessly I acted on the preset path of my life – studious boy to engineer to MBA to corporate hotshot to, ideally, retiree with money. Perhaps I told Vijayalaxmi what I did only to feel the weight of choosing something, to feel a sense of consequence.

No, that's not true. Or, is it?

'What are you thinking?' Jyoti asks me.

'You know, Jyoti, I could very easily have become a LOE,' I say. 'Or someone like a LOE.'

'Meaning?'

'Physics, chemistry, maths took me out of Muzaffarnagar, you know? Had I been bad at studies, had I taken a misstep somewhere, had my parents not been adamant about offering me the best education they could, had my parents not had enough to do any of these things then I could easily be sitting at an insurance branch somewhere, checking documents.'

'I think most people can build a narrative like that,' says Jyoti. 'It's like saying if things weren't OK, they would be not OK.'

'Can you? Can you build a narrative like that? Your life's journey is from Colaba to Malad, Jyoti. And you can always go back to Colaba. You know that.'

'Ouch, that hurts.'

'OK, that was harsh. Sorry.'

'Yeah.'

'Actually, I've nothing to reproach you with. You're so… you're so… aware. More than me for sure.'

'I'm just amazed how insensitive people can be,' says Jyoti. 'That Mitesh, for example. What a fucking ignoramus. It's as if he's decided to have a jihad against reason.'

'Yeah… Anyway, I'm sorry. I don't think I knew what I was trying to say.'

Jyoti puts her face on my shoulder, kisses it. We don't say anything for what seems like a long time. Then I pick up my phone and open the WhatsApp group *BLIC LOEs TOGETHER!!* There are ninety-eight unread messages there.

I tell the LOEs the truth. It takes three repetitions for the group members to stop seeking clarifications. At first I think it is because of the complexity of my words, or my inability to go beyond euphemism – *your services will no longer be required*; *the role will cease to exist*; *you will be laid off*. But then I realize that it might just be a case of denial. One of the LOEs actually tries to reason why it cannot happen. According to him, the role cannot be dissolved because LOEs do all the essential tasks in a branch, *things which HO people don't have the faintest clue about*. At least four people agree with him effusively with thumbs-up signs and tearing-up-laughing emojis. Another LOE requests the group not to be silly, to remember that the HO is powerful and can do whatever it wants. He further asks the group to refrain from speaking badly about HO people because I – *Saransh sir* – am also from HO. Immediately after him, someone adds a line in a different language. I translate it: *HO people ask the most stupid questions, that is true :P*. I have an impulse to answer with a smiley, but I rein it in.

New people are now getting added to the group every minute. For the benefit of the newcomers, my texts are copied and pasted repeatedly. Someone asks why I am telling this bad news to the LOEs. Someone else speculates that it is because I am leaving the company. I clarify that I'm not leaving the company. This leads to three people asking me again as to why I am revealing the truth. I decide to answer, and it is while I am typing in the answer that my own reasons become somewhat clearer to me.

> *I'm telling you because I think that what the company is doing is wrong. I'm telling you so as to give you an early warning. I've met many of you in person. I have an idea about how this will affect you. I hope this announcement gives you time to find an alternate opportunity. Please understand that I'm doing this in a personal capacity. No one from HO has asked me to share this information and I derive no personal benefit from it. In fact, I'm doing it at a considerable risk. I therefore request you to handle this information with care.*

My statement is followed by a flurry of responses:

Sir, how do you know about it?
Which team is responsible for this project, sir?
Arre he is part of this project!! He is also involved. Let's please confirm this first. Please don't trust him.
He was doing interviews for this only.
I think the people he met are the only people he's talking about.

Between all this incoming on the group, I receive three individual messages, each one asking the same question: *Are the interviewed candidates safe?* One of them is Raja from Hyderabad-1. I say *No* to each. I tell them that the interviews conducted by me or other HO people were all part of the project. This, of course, informs them of my direct involvement in enabling this situation. Like a hot potato, this information is immediately dumped in the group.

As soon as it becomes clear that the interviews conducted by the HO team, including me, were connected to the project of firing LOEs, volleys of abuse begin to fly. Someone named Sonu calls me a snake in Hindi. Three people start discussing between themselves as to why I disclosed the information to Vijayalaxmi. It is surmised that I developed a special liking for her during my short time in Hyderabad. I'm sure Vijayalaxmi is seeing this. But I'm also sure that she will remain silent, even as the innuendo regarding me and her intensifies. Out of the blue, Aanand from Chennai-1 abuses George Iype in Tamil, calling him a lecher and other nastier names, and also suggesting that female LOEs will now have even more reason to speak the truth about him. A couple of incredulous people ask if George is involved in all this. Someone reminds the group that George was involved with the interviews, too, which makes the group swiftly conclude that George has become a *Vibhishan* since his transfer to Mumbai. It is then suggested that the correct word in George's case would be *Judas*. By now an unsaid protocol has been established – anyone posting for the first time introduces himself/herself with his/her first name and branch location. Shwetank from Nagpur writes: *Actually I will tell you what happened. Saranshji got emotional with Vijayalaxmiji and told her about his project, but when Vijayalaxmiji started telling others, Saranshji thought he should become Mahatma Gandhi*. This is responded to with all kinds of cheering and approbation. What Shwetank has said is probably true to some degree. I did get emotional, though not *with* Vijayalaxmi. *Please don't talk about Vijayalaxmi with bad ideas*, Chandrasekhar from Hyderabad-1 says, standing up for his branch colleague. Several people support Chandrasekhar's request. Inside of a minute there is a consensus established – nobody will speak of Vijayalaxmi in all this.

Kasim from Bangalore-2 says that I might be someone from a competing organization trying to spread a rumour inside BLIC. His comment is immediately drowned in ridicule. Loveena from Nashik, the first woman to post anything on the group, writes a long message:

Saransh sir,

I don't know if you remember me. You interviewed me in Nashik. I told you about how we are derisking NRI cases. You were so happy to learn that, I remember. I just want to ask you why you and your friend from HO lied during the interview? You told me the interview was about improving the systems that I am using. You talked so nicely and now you are telling this news. If you speak truth the first time, I would not have talked to you at all. This is very bad. And now you're acting like you're neither in Congress nor in BJP.

What Loveena has said elicits a surge of support from others, with the Congress-BJP comment drawing specific approval. I think about whether I should say sorry for my dithering, for continuing to be a part of the lie until it was too late.

Michael from Panjim asks me to explain how exactly will HO automate the task of so many LOEs across the country. Shravan from Ludhiana questions if interviews were conducted only to make fun of LOEs.

'What's happening?' Jyoti asks, poking my shoulder.

'Mayhem,' I say. 'Let's go to the hotel.'

We get up from the bed and wear our clothes. The sandwiches remain uneaten. I put my phone in my bermudas' pocket. We walk to the house with Jyoti suggesting a return to the beach in the evening. Once inside she goes straight to the bathroom for a shower. I lie down on the bedroom floor and look at my phone's screen again.

More than fifty people, it seems, have been added to the group in the ten minutes it took us to move from the canopy bed on the beach to our room. My original message has been copied several times. The same questions are being asked again, but now group veterans have started responding to these questions. Some people are joking about me running away in terror. *I think someone has automated Saransh sir's job.* There are four missed calls on my phone, all from unknown numbers.

On the group it is now quite difficult to follow things. There are threads of non-sequitur conversations going on in various languages. Scrolling up and down, I notice that Manohar from Mumbai-4 has said that they (the LOEs) should treat me like a friend. *Saransh sir is our only friend and guide now.* I reply to that comment with a thank you. Manohar takes well to that and reminds the group that the truth would have remained hidden till the very last day had I not told it to Vijayalaxmi. Once again, several LOEs start joking that perhaps I only wanted to tell Vijayalaxmi. *Now he's in a good mess*, Guddu from Hyderabad-2 says, and many others share laughing emojis. Someone then shares a meme with text in Kannada.

I want to answer the questions raised by Loveena and Michael, I type in.

Please, sir, we are listening, Manohar says.

Please give gyan, sir. Aur kya denge, Guddu says.

Loveena, I lied during the interview because it was my job to lie at that time. It still is. We've been working on this project for almost a year now. It is only after the interviews started to happen, and when I began to meet the LOEs, that

I started to feel that this is wrong. But even then I didn't want to tell anyone. The truth is that I told Vijayalaxmi out of an impulse. I hadn't thought it through when I told her. It was a spur of the moment decision. Even earlier today, I didn't know if I wanted to share the truth with all of you. But I've taken that decision now. That's all I have to say in my defence. I'm sorry for not being able to see this from your perspective earlier.

Michael, the project uses computational methods broadly referred to as Machine Learning. Roughly put, all the decisions taken by the LOEs over the years are fed to a computer, which learns from these and is eventually able to take decisions like the LOEs. We tested it the first time in April this year. And we failed. Simply because there exists a lot of variation in how different branches go about executing different processes. You know that, I'm sure. We at the HO didn't know the extent of it. We did the interviews so that we could learn process variations at the branch level. The information obtained from the interviews is being used to improve the machine's decisions. And I can say that this time it won't fail.

There are a couple of cynical comments after my reply to Loveena, but after my reply to Michael, there is silence in the group for a full two minutes.

So each time we told you something unique about our branch, we were helping you steal our jobs? Michael asks.

Yes.

Santosh from Rourkela tells the group that he's checked my LinkedIn profile and has discovered that I'm a *product* of IIM Ahmedabad. Some praises of the institute and its *product* are then sung. Girish from Mumbai-3 comments that it is obvious that something so technical requires someone with *a good brain*. This benign turn in the conversation baffles me; it seems that by briefly touching upon the methodology, I've impressed some LOEs with the *science* needed to take away their jobs.

Jyoti comes out of the bathroom. 'How's it going?' she asks.

'I don't know,' I say. 'I don't know what is going to happen.'

'Go, take a shower,' she says. 'Take a break from the phone. I have something to tell you.'

'I don't think I can take a break right now.'

'You look worried,' she says.

'That's because I am worried,' I say.

'About what?'

'About… I don't know, Jyoti. These people are asking all these questions. And I can't stop answering. And each time I answer I grow a little more scared. See, someone is calling me right now.'

I sit up on the floor and cancel the call. Jyoti sits on the bed, just behind me, and holds my head in her hands. She starts to massage it. 'What are you scared of?' she asks.

'Each answer of mine is written proof,' I say. 'There are two hundred people in this group now. By tomorrow, everyone in the company will know what I've done.'

'Show me what's happening.'

I hand the phone to Jyoti. She continues to massage my head with one hand while checking the phone with the other.

'There is someone asking you if there is a technical way to stop the machine,' she says. 'You should think of that, shouldn't you?'

'I don't know how that can be done. Maybe our data scientist does. Or the IT people. But there is no way they will do that, of course. What else?'

'Well... a long message. Someone saying that he's worked in this job for eleven years and that he knows that no other insurance company pays as much money to the LOE job profile as your company does. He says losing this job means accepting a 20 to 30 per cent pay cut. Someone else stressing that this cut is only for the few among them who can find jobs in time. Then someone saying that he's planned his sister's wedding next year and may have to reconsider it. Then someone asking if anyone in the group has contacts of HR people in any insurance company in Kolkata. Then...'

'OK, stop, please.'

'Yeah, OK,' Jyoti says. Then, after about a minute of silence: 'Actually, there is something I wanted to talk to you about.'

'That you're pregnant? And the child is not mine?'

'No, you bastard.'

'Then later, maybe? Please?'

Jyoti massages my head for five more minutes after which I lie down on the bed with her and start reading the messages in *BLIC LOEs Together!!* again. There are numerous personal situations mentioned, each one dire in its own way, each one proving how essential the job is to the LOEs. Some Area Operations Managers (AOMs) – LOEs' bosses – have also joined the group. Two of them have written individually to me, posing the question that if the LOE role is going to go then is the company looking to transition AOMs in new roles. I know that most of the AOMs are going to lose their jobs, too. The fact that the information has moved upwards in the operations hierarchy – from LOEs to AOMs – makes it crystal clear to me that no part of what I've done in this group will remain hidden. In fact, there is a high chance that powers at the HO are beginning to be informed about what has happened. And what has happened is, for all practical purposes, professional harakiri on my part.

I continue to receive calls from unknown numbers; I continue to drop them. On the group there are several people asking me to stop the machine, to somehow impede its learning process. Mayur from Pune-2 opines that if the machine is learning from his decisions, then he will start taking wrong decisions now. He will reject the applications that need to be accepted and accept the applications that need to be rejected. Several people ask me if this approach will work. It is something Rizwan can answer best. Theoretically, if all the LOEs started taking adverse decisions right now there will definitely be an aberration – a silent one, with no alarms ringing – in the machine's learning process. Either Rizwan will detect this contamination or he will not. If he does, he should be able to re-tune the machine either by finding a pattern in the contamination or by simply choosing to ignore any new incoming data (the machine has already consumed piles of anomaly-free historical data and its algorithms are robust by now). In case Rizwan does not detect it (the likelier scenario in my understanding), the company – unaware of this silent rebellion of the LOEs – will continue with its plan. In either case, the LOEs will lose their jobs.

I write: *It is too late now to do what Mayur is suggesting.*

OK, sir, very helpful of you, Mayur replies.

A discussion premised on the fact that the company still needs LOEs until April then ensues. There is talk of a non-cooperation movement. Various options are discussed – to not come to the branch, to take mass leaves, to strike, to go to Mumbai and express displeasure. The sudden escalation in intent frightens me. But what else did I think would happen?

'I don't know what the LOEs will do now,' I tell Jyoti, who, like me, has been looking into her phone for the past few minutes. 'They are talking about collective action. Sounds like there will be some sort of unionizing.'

'They will do what they think they have to do, Saransh. Your role in all this is actually over.'

'What has been my role in all this, remind me?' I say.

We shift and turn sideways to face each other. 'You're the source,' she says. 'And you're the sauce,' she adds with a laugh.

I laugh, too, albeit a bit hesitant. 'I'm the source that initiated the project. I'm the source that ruined the project.'

'If you initiated it, it was always yours to destroy.'

'I'll get fired, you know? The LOEs will get fired. The agitating ones among them will be fired much before April. Maybe the SPG will be dismantled. Maybe the buck will move up to Unnikrishnan's level. Maybe he will be fired, too. No one comes out of it better than yesterday.'

'Are you scared of getting fired? You will find something else. Even I did.'

'You did? What do you mean?'

'That's what I've been wanting to talk to you about. I got a job,' Jyoti says.

'That's great news,' I say, 'that's really great news, Jyoti.' I caress her hair with my fingers and place my thumb on her cheekbone. 'What kind of job is it?'

'A longform magazine, kind of like The New Yorker. The AsiaPlus newspaper group is setting it up so the pay is going to be good.'

'So you get to write?'

'Yes, I'm hired as a staff writer.'

'Wow. When do you join?'

'It's in Delhi. I join in a week from now.'

'Delhi?'

'Yes.'

'You're going to Delhi?'

'The job is in Delhi.'

'But I'm in Mumbai.'

'So?'

'So?'

'Saransh, be real.'

'Be real?'

'Yes! I don't know what's changing your facial expression. But you cannot realistically expect me to forgo an offer like this just to be close to you.'

'What can I expect, then? When did you apply to this? Why didn't you tell me?'

'I didn't tell you because I thought I wouldn't get it. And also because it never crossed my mind that I must.'

'Just last night you told me that you are free-riding for now.'

'I didn't know until last night. And, anyway, I didn't say I was free-riding with pleasure. I don't want to depend on my father, Saransh. He makes money from evil clients. And I want to do good work. Can't you come to Delhi? You just said you're going to be fired.'

There is a casualness in Jyoti's tone – about me and her, and about my job – that I find alarming. I get up from the bed and start pacing about the room. 'How can you do this to me?' I say.

'Hey, don't be a dick now,' says Jyoti, suddenly kneeling on the bed and pointing a finger at me. 'I'm not married to you. I can go wherever the fuck I want.'

I look at her stunned. 'But we're together, aren't we? Boyfriend–girlfriend, remember? What if I can't come to Delhi? All the good financial sector jobs are in Mumbai.'

'If you can't come to Delhi we will see if this can work long distance.'

'And if it doesn't?'

'If it doesn't, it doesn't, Saransh. For fuck's sake, what do you want me to do? Take a vow that I'll be with you forever and ever, even if my own life is taking me elsewhere?'

'It is just the sex for you, isn't it?' I say.

'Stop saying stupid things.'

'What is the smart thing to say right now?'

'That you're happy for me.'

I stop and kneel on the bed like Jyoti. We are facing each other. I hold her by her shoulders and stare into her eyes. 'I love you,' I say softly.

Jyoti breaks into a confused smile. Then she hugs me. I understand it as her way to avoid looking into my eyes, to avoid saying *I love you, too*. I stroke her back. We are in a conciliatory embrace. But in the next few seconds conciliation begins to morph into desire.

We make love at a slow pace, our slowest ever. No words, not even any sounds of pleasure. At the end of it, I feel disoriented as I would if I woke up in a place different from the one I slept in. We wipe our genitals using the tissue roll kept on a bedside table for exactly this purpose. We don't have anything to say to each other. Jyoti closes her eyes, as if willing herself to sleep. I pick up my phone. There are three missed calls from Mitesh. There is a message from him too.

> *WHAT THE FUCK are you doing, you moron!! You're destroying all our hard work. Trust me this will have consequences. Switch off your phone RIGHT NOW if you want to have any chance. I told you this Jyoti woman is going to be bad for you.*

I switch off my phone in sadness more than in fear. I feel like crying. I feel like repeating 'I love you' to Jyoti, even if in vain.

I take my naked self to the bathroom.

UNNIKRISHNAN

THE PHONE STAYS SWITCHED-OFF DURING THE REST OF THE Goa vacation. Slowly my anxiety about the LOE situation ebbs. I notice the taste differentials in beers of different brands, play frisbee with the teenaged children of the big family, make love with Jyoti, light diyas along the balcony railing on the day before Diwali, cook a delicious chicken curry – and there is more of me present in each of these things. Suddenly exempted from the need to impress, reveal, conceal or entertain, my interactions with Jyoti have a calmness about them, and somehow this elevates their depth and quality. It definitely makes her more candid. She tells me how her parents always wanted her to study law and how she managed to wriggle out of that preordained path. She tells me how moving out of her Colaba house signified freedom for her. She tells me how she is a bit worried about shifting to Delhi, 'that hellhole for single working women.' I do not react to the Delhi apprehensions or the word *single*. I speak, instead, of my perfect childhood, 'etched in my mind like a Malgudi-type idyll.' I tell her of evening games of cricket, of bathing under tube wells, of cycling to school on foggy mornings. Jyoti speculates about how my perception of my own childhood contributed to my feeling the way I do about Alan Kurdi. I reject this theory politely, but my rejection somehow initiates a discussion on society's desensitization to violence, a discussion that spills from dinner that night onto breakfast the following morning. And even further. At one point, I mention that human civilization is actually in its least-violent-ever phase. This makes Jyoti opine that our collective desensitization is not to acts of violence *here*, but to reports and images of acts of violence *elsewhere*. 'And *here* is constricting because we have lesser and lesser amounts of attention to pay to things around us.' We circle back to Alan Kurdi and acknowledge that the images of his dead body have a power that contradicts what Jyoti has said. The event has happened elsewhere but it affects us here. At least a few of us.

That our conversation never becomes an argument is not lost on me. Earlier, Jyoti would have found a way to steer the conversation towards my work in BLIC and I would have tried to defend my position. That route has become impossible; now it is Jyoti who wears the mantle of nodding at capitalism.

On our penultimate day in Goa, while watching the final sunset together, I venture to say that in our beleaguered times it is images like Alan Kurdi's that have to do the work of art. Jyoti asks me if I'm in my *Given Eichmann is guilty* mode and laughs. I do not laugh with her. I look at the sun – red, reddening, about to touch the straight line of the horizon – and speak about how a child's body is something that we all have memories of interacting with. 'Pinching the cheeks… or carrying the child such that the hip rests on our arm and our other hand holds the back… like this… or messing with the hair… or holding the small fingers… or having the small fingers hold our fingers. We know the child's body in comparison to ours – more beautiful than ours, more fragile than ours, needing more care. We know that a child's body is sacred. On some level, in fact, I would even say that we know it as the *only* sacred thing.'

I go on to point out how, in the photo, Alan Kurdi's body is neither mangled with injury nor straightened like how a body packed in a coffin would be. It is intact, and it is in a unique posture. 'The intactness and the posture… these things fire our memories… memories of interacting with a child's body. We are almost physically jolted when we see the photo… why?... Because our own body is remembering another fragile body… it is telling us that that body is alive, that that body needs to be picked up. But our mind knows that it is dead. What follows is that microsecond of denial when our body and our mind contradict each other. Then the mind takes over, of course, and we feel angry… why? … Because something sacred has been violated.'

The sun has dipped into the sea completely. The point where the sun has dipped is now sucking all the remaining light in the sky. 'And that's how it does the work of art?' Jyoti asks.

'Yes.'

Jyoti then remarks on the type of anger I ended at and calls it 'too pure, too irrational'. According to her, this anger allows for an interpretation in which all the grown men drowning in the Mediterranean are nothing compared to one Alan Kurdi. 'I think there is another contradiction that plays out after the raw anger you talk of,' she says, 'between the less-than-conscious mind and the rational mind. And the latter wins eventually, of course. We link the child's death to abstract ideas – the evils of war, the refugee crisis, the shittiness of this shitty world. We try and make sense of it.'

'Yes, our anger becomes less pure, more functional,' I say.

The sky darkens suddenly. We stand up and dust the sand off our clothes. I think of Jyoti's anger towards capitalism and the impurities in it.

'That's how you survive,' she says, as if answering my thoughts instead of what I've said.

We return to Mumbai on Sunday evening. Jyoti spends the night at my place but leaves for her apartment early in the morning. She hasn't taken her toothbrush, I notice.

It is during the auto ride to Bansal Towers that I switch my phone on for the first time in days. There are hundreds of messages on the LOE group. I mute it. There are messages from my mother asking me why I kept my phone switched off during Diwali. I fabricate a reason and apologize to her. Then there are messages from Mitesh. In one, he tells me how on Wednesday, the day before Diwali,

George Iype had two new cases of sexual harassment filed against him. In a later message, he tells me that this time the CASH committee is going to terminate George and that I'd do better not to cross his path on Monday. His last message has him telling me how I've ruined everyone's Diwali, and how I am a chutiya of the highest order.

After WhatsApp I check my work inbox. There is an email with the subject line *SPG Confidential Info Leak* from Manpreet. Even before clicking it open my vision constricts and my throat turns dry. I realize that I fear how things will play out from here.

Dear Saransh Malik,

This email is with regard to two recent incidents involving some Local Operations Executives (LOEs) in the South Zone.

To know the incidents being referred to, please see the details provided below:

1. On 17 and 18 October 2017, 17 LOEs from our branches in Telangana and Andhra Pradesh went on simultaneous sick leaves. This brought to a standstill almost all business-related activities at the respective branches. The direct money impact of this abstention is estimated to be INR 34,00,000. Such behaviour has never been observed in any organization in the insurance sector in India and has thus brought considerable disrepute to BLIC in these states. The company is taking steps to ensure that such actions are not repeated. The company is also considering disciplinary action against the concerned LOEs.

2. On 17 October 2017, 7 LOEs from our branches in Kerala approached a prominent political party in the state and became its members. On behalf of the LOEs the party forwarded an indefinite strike notice dated 18 October 2017 to our head office in Mumbai. These LOEs demand termination of employment with a net severance package of INR 6,00,000 per person, which amounts to upwards of INR 42,00,000. The direct financial impact due to the strike and the subsequent loss of business is estimated to be INR 26,00,000 at this point. This number is bound to increase. The strike threatens the viability of BLIC operations in the state, thereby jeopardizing the livelihoods of the other 34 BLIC employees there.

These events have had a damaging impact on the organization's reputation. They have also endangered the success of a critical project of the Special Projects Group. You are a member of the SPG. It has been established that both incidents were caused by the LOEs' fears of country-wide layoffs.

Under the guidance of BLIC top management, the SPG has been allowed to work on a project to automate parts of the LOE work profile using Machine Learning and other latest technologies. The company's pursuit of this and other such projects is to develop high-end capabilities in light of the advancements in the external technological environment. The company has made no official communication regarding the expiry of the LOE role, and therefore considers any comments to that effect, especially those made outside official channels, as rumours.

It has been established that sometime in mid-October, you revealed details of your project to a LOE in Hyderabad. Thereafter, you joined an informal WhatsApp group on 16 October and shared information regarding the SPG project. The group consisted of more than 200 LOEs at the time, some of whom subsequently caused the two incidents mentioned above. You also shared with the LOEs your belief that the SPG project will lead to terminations in April 2018. Moreover, you discussed ways of sabotaging the project with the LOEs.

It has also been reported that you have shared details of the SPG project, including the misleading implication that it will lead to layoffs, to your personal relations outside the organization.

As a member of the SPG and a key participant of the said project, your conduct is deemed to be in violation of the BLIC Code of Conduct for Employees (CCE), which was signed by you on the day of your joining the company. (In case you wish to, you can avail a scanned copy of your signed CCE document through the HR portal.)

This email is to inform you of the disciplinary committee formed to further investigate your involvement in the incidents. The committee includes Mr Adarsh Unnikrishnan (Head, Digital Transformation & Special Projects Group), Mr Suresh Jain (Head, Strategy) and Ms Manpreet Kaur (DVP, HR). After due meetings with you and other stakeholders involved, the committee will arrive at a decision regarding your employment with BLIC and the terms thereof, as necessary. The decision of the committee will be final and without the possibility of appeal. The schedule for its meetings will be communicated to you in a separate email.

Until the committee concludes its inquiry, you are demanded to vacate your seat inside the SPG sitting area (Meeting Room–Zepellin) and seat yourself in your assigned cubicle in the common area in Zone 2. The network access in your laptop has been restricted to LOCAL and your email rights have been restricted to READ ONLY, meaning that you will only be able to access intranet facilities and not be able to send emails to recipients inside or outside BLIC.

In case you resign before the committee arrives at a decision, you will be required to serve a notice period of three months as per your appointment letter, during which time the committee will continue its work. (In case you wish to, you can avail a scanned copy of your signed appointment letter through the HR portal.)

As a member of the committee, I advise you to respond to its questions with utmost honesty.

Regards,

Manpreet Kaur,
Deputy Vice President,
Human Resources - Corporate Office,
Bansal Life Insurance Company

I have a flurry of thoughts after reading the email.

1. That's it? That's all that happened? Only 24 LOEs acted? What happened to the rest?
2. Is this the company denying that it wanted to fire the LOEs?
3. If the LOEs create a situation in which the company has to respond to their queries, will the company maintain this denial?
4. If the company maintains the denial then surely it cannot reverse it. Certainly, the project will be dead then.
5. Whatever happens, my BLIC career is over.

Zeppelin is Zepellin again. The sheet bearing the corrected spelling has been removed. I step inside; everyone is present. At once, George rises from his seat and lunges towards me. 'You bastard,' he shouts. Rizwan and Sayantan restrain him from hitting me.

'I'm just here to get my stuff,' I point to the drawer next to the TV. My office laptop and some personal items are stored there.

'You'll rot in hell, you bhenchod,' George shouts again.

'Please, George,' Mitesh says stiffly.

'You've risked our professional lives, Saransh. You had no right to,' Ankita says.

This makes me laugh.

'Why are you laughing?' Ankita asks.

'Because he is a self-destructive moron,' Mitesh butts in.

'I'm laughing at how spectacularly obtuse you are, Ankita,' I say.

'Obtuse? What obtuse? Don't speak to me like that,' Ankita warns me.

'Fair,' I say, 'then don't speak to me at all.' I take out my things and put them in a bag. Just as I'm leaving the room, Mitesh says, 'We're all waiting for what Unni does to you.'

I take my seat inside my designated cubicle, switch my laptop on, and check my emails. There are a few emails from LOEs asking me questions similar to the ones on the WhatsApp group. In one of them, a LOE tells me of his daughter who is suffering from leukemia. He asks me if I can help financially.

Just then my cubicle's landline phone rings. Someone's just dialed the wrong extension number, I think. But then I see Manpreet's name on the display. This call is for me.

'Hi, Saransh, how are you?' the voice on the phone asks me. It isn't Manpreet's.

'I'm fine... Who is this?'

'This is Unnikrishnan.'

'Oh, sir...'

'I'm very curious, Saransh,' Unnikrishnan says, and then pauses, as if his declaration of curiosity is in itself a thing to be acknowledged.

'About?' I ask.

'About the entire affair with the LOEs. I was wondering if you and I could talk.'

'Sure, sir. Is this the committee thing?'

'Oh, no, no. The committee business will be handled in its own sweet time. I was just hoping for a brief, informal chat. Could you come to my cabin? Say, now?'

'Sure, sir. I'm not busy at all.'

Standing up I can see Manpreet's cubicle and Unnikrishnan standing beside it. He is gaunt, in his early fifties, with a head of mostly white hair that greatly enhances his wise-man appeal, which is also added to, I must say, by a certain economy in movement. I raise my hand diminutively to acknowledge him; he smiles professionally and turns around. He walks towards his cabin, which happens to be on the far side of the zone. I leave my cubicle and follow him. For some reason, I'm struck by memories of how measured and shrewd he used to be during our SCOM meetings – those are my defining images of him. He was totally unlike his peers who, deficient in understanding the technicalities of SPG projects, often ended up making a virtue of going further down the details, details that confounded them at each step until things reached a point where their helplessness ran the risk of betraying itself. The only possible action thereafter was to order more coffee or share a joke about a secretary or utter some platitudes about how deeply the devil is embedded in the details and why they ask what they ask because that's their role in the whole game. Unnikrishnan never participated in that badminton; he granted himself altitude, made himself the guardian of the big picture. He understood tech and its potentialities and had an innate knack for simplifying things. His queries were never trivial, of course, and always related to outcomes.

As I approach his cabin, I remember how I always felt that he liked me, how he saw me as someone sharing some traits with him – the ability to use frameworks to think through something new, the ability to form a decision tree in the head, the ability to articulate clearly. I had probably developed this notion because Unnikrishnan, after the commencement of iBlink, had often directed his toughest questions towards me. This sort of elevated me in the eyes of other SPG members, too. 'My head feels light when Unni and Saransh get talking,' Poonam had once said after one such meeting. I used to think that I could, one day, be him.

And now, in circumstances quite different for both of us, we are going to talk again. I would be lying if I said I am not nervous. This is the first time I'll meet him alone, without the rest of the SPG. Only Mitesh gets to meet Unnikrishnan one-to-one.

I knock on the glass door once and enter his cabin. He removes his gray blazer and places it languidly over the shoulders of his chair – the relatively plush piece of furniture given to all cabin-holders, finished with glossy imitation-leather and armed with the capability to stiffen, loosen, swivel, shorten, et cetera. The chair he offers me is more mundane, of the common variety ubiquitous in the office. I sit down. He nods once. Then he sits down on his chair and turns it 180 degrees, effectively turning his back to me. On his work desk, he opens his laptop and starts to scroll slowly through his inbox. His cabin is like every other cabin in the office – a long L-shaped desk attached to two adjoining walls, storage drawers below the desk, glass slabs for show items above it, a translucent board riveted to the third wall for scribbling ideas, a steel holder for dusters and markers attached next to the glass board, three chairs in all, with two of the common variety facing *the seat*, and a small round table daintily filling up the awkwardness in between. In his case, the glass slabs above the desk give space to framed photographs featuring him as he felicitates someone or is himself felicitated at functions inside or outside the company. The photographs are surrounded by big and small trophies. There is one picture of his wife and his daughter, but that is placed close to his laptop on the desk. The fact that Unnikrishnan was curious about me minutes ago and now ignores me doesn't bother me. I see it as far too typical of senior-management behaviour to mind. I concentrate on the only thing drawn on the glass board – a two-by-two matrix whose horizontal side is labelled *Effort*, low to high, and whose vertical side is labelled *Impact*, low to high. Four words are placed in the space created by these two perpendicular lines, the dots connecting them forming a straight forty-five-degree line outwards: *Digitization*, *Digitalization*, *High-end Automation*, *Transformation*. *High-end Automation* is circled. That's probably where Unnikrishnan thinks we are at right now, one step away from *Transformation*.

Finally, Unnikrishnan turns his chair to face me. 'Sorry, Saransh,' he says, 'I wanted to chat with you at leisure so I thought I might as well clear a couple of pending items before we start.'

'Yeah, no problem, sir.'

'Well… there is one thing I have to ask you… this is informal, you understand?'

'Yes, sir.'

'So, could you just show me the apps running on your phone once? And then allow me to place it on the table?'

The request perplexes me for a second, but then I realize that this is Unnikrishnan taking precaution. So, perhaps, calling me from Manpreet's desk was the first precaution. And now, he wants to ensure that there is no record of this conversation, nothing on my phone at least. I do as I am told. 'Should I… should I insist on something like that too?' I ask uneasily.

Unnikrishnan laughs in response. His laughter is a bit gravelly. 'Of course, of course,' he says. 'Here… as I said, this is informal, and the stupid thing with the phones is only to ensure that we keep it so.'

'Yes, sir.'

'So, tell me, are you against automation as a… as a… concept? Or was your action a spur of the moment thing?'

'Sir?'

'Was your action based on the belief that we must not automate things? Or was it just because you were angry about some small thing? The small thing could be anything, of course. Something rude that was said to you by someone. Or a colleague's general behaviour. The stress inside that room where all you SPG folks are camped in. I imagine it can be quite exhausting in there.'

I take a moment to think about it. 'A bit of both, I think,' I say.

'A bit of both,' repeats Unnikrishnan. He has a mild smile on his face. 'It interests me to know about both then.'

I try to smile in return.

'Look, Saransh, I have a twenty-five-year long career,' he says. 'I have seen all kinds of employee behaviour. Insubordination, recklessness, even criminal behaviour. In that sense, nothing surprises me. But I guess what piques my interest here is the peculiar nature of what we, as a company, are trying to do with iBlink – its uniqueness, so to speak – and, in that respect, the uniqueness of what you did.'

He pauses, the smile on his face morphing into an inquiring expression. An inquiry of my face.

He starts again: 'Automation – and I have been thinking about this for a long time – is the great goal of business enterprise, isn't it? Running a business with the least amount of resources. The holy grail of Capitalism, if I may. And fighting against it is a sign of a sort of… a sort of… I guess… Socialism. You understand what I'm saying? You understand these terms?'

'I understand these terms quite well, sir.'

'I thought so. Anyway… we will go into these things later. First tell me what made you do what you did. What was the trigger?'

'You could say the trigger was an argument with Mitesh,' I say.

'In the office?'

'At his house.'

'Interesting. What was it about?'

'About things that had nothing to do with our project. Actually, he had an argument with my girlfriend. It was a Sunday lunch thing at his place that got… not ugly… but yeah it couldn't remain very friendly either.'

'OK. He did mention your girlfriend. But not this lunch meeting.'

'How then?' I ask.

'He talked to me last week. I think he was being careful after the leak. Keeping the company's interests in mind. He said you'd told your girlfriend about the project and that it was risky because she is a journalist with a… with a certain ideology.'

I shake my head in exasperation. 'I met Mitesh's wife at his house, sir,' I say, 'and I think she knows, too. Now, she works in a general insurance company that also has a life insurance arm. She wouldn't even need to be of a certain ideology to cause us harm. I mean… Mitesh's wife has a clear connection with a direct competitor. My girlfriend, on the other hand, was not even a practising journalist when I told her. I think I should bring this point out in the official committee meeting as well. This whole *Saransh told his girlfriend and she's a communist* angle is bullshit. Sorry to use the word.'

'It is bullshit,' says Unnikrishnan, though the word does not seem natural coming from him. 'I tell my wife many things. We are not in the secret services or anything.' He smiles again, eliciting a tic from my face as well. 'Anyway, given what happened that day, how did it come to a point where you ended up telling a LOE that she might be losing her job? Someone named Vijayalaxmi, I'm told.'

'Vijayalaxmi had been asking me for a transfer to Mumbai for personal reasons. She happened to follow up with me that Sunday, right after we left Mitesh's house. And I happened to tell her that there was no point in seeking this transfer because she'd be fired anyway.'

'Happened to tell… hmm,' he nods slowly. Then, looking down at the round table between us, 'Had you been feeling guilty about doing the project?'

My first reaction to the question is to be impressed with Unnikrishnan. I realize I won't be able to lie. 'Yes, I was,' I say.

'Why?'

'I don't know. I haven't been able to completely process it.'

'Try,' he says. 'And, please, this is an informal meeting. There is no wrong answer.'

'I…' I find it difficult to speak.

'You know, Saransh, we are having this conversation because I like you. I know you've been running the show in that room. Mitesh told me about the solution you proposed for the underwriting project. That's what I would normally quote as an example of genius in management. Mitesh does what he does, sure, but it's you who conceives things, who solves conceptual problems while keeping the real world in mind. I know that. And that means the company knows that. You're a very valuable resource. We wouldn't want to lose you.'

'I was feeling guilty because I was having doubts,' I say.

'Doubts about?'

'I was not sure it was right. Eliminating jobs, I mean. Especially in this depersonalized, devious sort of way.'

'Hmm…'

'That scrutiny job that our LOEs do, it is strenuous, it requires concentration. They've been doing it for us for years. When we suddenly automate it, in a way we prove to them that what they did was always insignificant. We take away their pride… their well-earned pride. You will remember, sir, the SPG started interviewing LOEs because in the first iteration the machine couldn't deal with local process variations. The term we used was *anomaly*. But for them… for the LOEs… these things are not anomalies, these are the best things about their job. It's their applied intelligence, manoeuvres that they have created locally to function in the absence of detailed instructions from the top. We will be doing something similar in the underwriting project as well. We will be automating jobs in which people have taken great pride and have made a virtue of their judgment capabilities.'

'True…'

'So, I was thinking, what is it that we really do? We meaning SPG. We come in, turn everything into statistics and level years of human expertise into the ground. And, frankly, we're never really sure the results will be better.'

'I'm afraid I'm going to have to ask – so what?' asks Unnikrishnan, the last two words delivered in a voice deeper than earlier.

'So what?' I repeat.

'Yes, so what?'

'I don't know. I guess there has to be a plan to absorb these people elsewhere. And maybe their welfare has to be built into the cost-benefit analysis somehow.'

'All right,' says Unnikrishnan. 'Have you seen the movie Moneyball? Brad Pitt?'

'Yes, I have,' I answer, already sensing where this is headed.

'At the heart of it, it's a machine beats man movie, no? At least I think of it that way. A predictive model does better scouting for baseball players than professional scouts. And these buggers have been doing it for years. How? Because the model can find patterns in performance data that a human mind cannot even begin to comprehend. I know that the movie simplifies and politicizes things a bit. The scouts are shown to be somewhat complacent, even biased – that's bullshit. The movie could have been even better if the scouts were shown to possess indisputable expertise, I think. Anyway, my question is, why should that baseball club continue to employ the scouts?'

'I don't think baseball clubs have stopped employing scouts after Moneyball.'

'You do get my point.'

'It all depends on what we are optimizing for, sir,' I say.

'Meaning?'

'If the baseball club were optimizing for cost, and the cost of prediction by a human was much higher than that by a machine, while the accuracies of both predictions were within an acceptable limit, then I guess the scouts would not be needed. But if the club were optimizing for accuracy of predictions then a machine plus man model might be better suited. Which is to say, a model in which the machine becomes an aid for the scouts.'

'But what value would a scout add in the machine plus man model?'

'The machine doesn't consider several attributes that a scout can – physicality, batting or bowling stance, family support system, reaction to pressure… did the player give a good performance when the fans were abusing him… and, if we were optimizing for marketing revenue, the looks of the player… his saleability. Theoretically, of course, we can imagine a machine model that takes into account these variables as well. But the data gathering process would be costly – it would practically involve employing people and systems that could turn out to be way more expensive than the scouts.'

Unnikrishnan inhales and exhales loudly, then slaps the round tabletop with his palm twice. 'That's why I like you,' he says.

For the first time in this room, I smile genuinely.

'But the scouts would have to accept a lower salary in a machine plus man model,' Unnikrishnan asserts.

He's right. I don't have a rejoinder to that. 'The world is a hard place, I get that.' I say.

'Do you want anything to drink?' Unnikrishnan asks. 'I'm thinking of coffee.'

'Yes, sir, black coffee would be good. Thanks.'

He turns in his chair, dials the four-digit pantry number on his landline, and asks for two cups of coffee in a soft voice. Then he turns back towards me and smiles professionally.

'This could be automated too, sir,' I say.

'The pantry service?'

'Yes.'

'I think the human solution is cheaper. For now.'

Pure reason, I think. That's what the two of us are faced with in this conversation. But is that what I want? I realize I don't, and at once my desire to be sharp and intelligent dissipates. I become freer in my head. 'I will take the liberty to say one thing,' I begin, coughing once, 'that the way things are done in the SPG – and I'm not saying that I've not contributed to it – is also a problem.'

'How so?'

'The SPG has understood its mandate as one that entails firing as many people as possible… and as quickly as possible. The business outcomes are a secondary concern. We identify a set of people whose work can be automated, with whatever degree of accuracy, and then we blindly set out to do it. It's become a kind of… a kind of…'

'Fetish?'

'Yeah. Fetish, yeah. I think that's the right word.'

'That's unavoidable in my view. This fetishized sense of purpose. This missionary zeal. Whatever you call it. People in my position would do anything to acquire teams with that mentality. I'm sure Mitesh leads the way here.'

'Yes, he does,' I say. 'My intention is not to criticize him, though.'

'I understand that.'

A young woman, dressed in a pair of black trousers and a white shirt, steps into the room after knocking twice. Her hands are clad in white gloves, which are stained in several places by tea and coffee spills. Gingerly she places our cups on the table. Unnikrishnan mutters multiple polite thank yous.

I pick up my cup. 'It's vulgar,' I say just before sipping my coffee. 'I find this zeal vulgar.'

'Vulgar?'

'Vulgar in the sense that… well… how do I say it? The SPG has dehumanized the whole process. We see numbers. We salivate at the salary cost we can save. We don't care for anything else. We don't suffer, so we see no suffering.'

'Would you rather suffer?'

'I am due some suffering,' I say, almost too cheekily. 'Now at least the company will make me suffer even if I fail to do it to myself.'

'I…' Unnikrishnan begins to speak, then shifts in his chair. That makes a strange hissing sound as air escapes from one side of the cushion. He wants to talk about something else. 'I don't see what your protest is, Saransh. Is it against automation? I know you are smart enough to know that it is unavoidable. Is it against the vulgarity of implementing it? That's a workplace thing that can be sorted out. We can systemize empathy and include it in the SPG's work processes. We can make sure that SPG people don't have to face the people they make irrelevant. What, then? Is your protest against the system itself? I want to know which system we are talking about. The system, as in SPG? The system, as in Bansal Life Insurance? The system, as in the life insurance industry? The system, as in the financial services sector? The system, as in, global Capitalism? Do you really know what is it that you want to change? Or what is it that you will definitely not accept?'

I am struck by the hint of emotion in his voice. I don't have an answer.

'Every new invention causes disruption,' Unnikrishnan continues. 'When mankind invented the wheel, some strong guys – the log lifters, I imagine – must have lost their jobs. When we invented the printing press, I'm sure numerous calligraphers and scribblers became irrelevant. With photography, portrait painters lost ground. The assembly line fucked a lot of industry workers. Computers, the internet – these things have changed the world too. The world moves forward, Saransh. And some people are left behind. The *system* that you find yourself protesting against – have you considered that it might be humanity itself?'

'And now we've invented intelligence,' I say, rhetorically, unsure of what point I make by saying that.

Unnikrishnan ignores the comment. 'And don't you – you, personally – benefit from the accumulation of these inventions?'

'I do.'

'So?'

'We can be better now, I think.'

'Better, *now*?'

'Better than we may have been. When I say *we*, I mean humans.'

'How so?'

'I don't know. But we ought to be better. We can cause less pain.'

'What would you do in our scenario? What would you do for the LOEs?'

'I would start a transition programme to reskill them, to put them in sales.'

Unnikrishnan snorts. 'And what would you do with the non-performers three months later?' he asks.

'I would continue to invest. Make the non-performers learn other skills.'

'That's impractical. And you know it.'

'I would give people a genuine chance, sir. That's my point.'

'Why? It doesn't make sense.'

'Because they are people,' I say, my voice rising.

Unnikrishnan leans back holding his coffee cup in his right hand. 'So guess I should give you a chance, too?'

'I can't decide for you,' I say, the anger quite clear in my voice.

He moves his left hand through his hair and lets out a short whistle. He closes and opens his eyes. 'Have you tried to sabotage the project in any technical way?' he asks me, his eyes now hardened as they look into mine.

'What do you mean?'

'You know what I mean.'

'I'm not the data scientist. Rizwan is. I'm not the one who controls what data is fed to the machine. I'm not the one who monitors the stats.'

'You're a grad from the best B-school in India. You're one of the most intelligent guys in BLIC, definitely the most intelligent in the SPG. It's not beyond you.'

'It is. Unless Rizwan is working with me on the conspiracy.' I speak the last word in a dramatic whisper.

'Is he?'

'Come on, Unni,' I say, addressing him by his nickname for the first time ever.

'Is he?'

'Is this what this conversation has been all about? You trying to decipher if I have done irreparable damage?'

'This is an informal conversation.'

'There is no technical plan to sabotage the project. Unless Rizwan is acting on his own.'

'Do you want Rizwan to act on his own?'

I shake my head. The word 'fuck' escapes my mouth. Unnikrishnan doesn't react to it. 'I don't want Rizwan to do anything other than his job,' I say.

'Fair enough,' says Unnikrishnan placing his cup back on the table. 'Manpreet's email is pretty clear… about the harm you've caused the company.'

'It is,' I say. I look straight into Unnikrishnan's eyes. I'm being defiant, I think.

'There is a direct monetary impact. And our progress in SPG may have been threatened too. Do you regret what you did?' he asks.

'Which part?'

'Well, let's say the part where you advised the LOEs about sabotaging the project.'

'I didn't do that. I, in fact, told them not to try.'

'Why were you so generous to BLIC?'

'I was not generous. I just knew it wouldn't work. Except perhaps delaying the inevitable by a month or so.'

'The *inevitable*,' notes Unnikrishnan. 'I like that. Anyway, there has been a fallout. Do you regret causing it?'

'Is my answer important?'

'Your employment with BLIC is in question, Saransh. What you say now might not be important, but if you go to the committee hearings feeling penitent, it will definitely improve your chances of staying on in the company.'

'And if I don't do that? If I don't feel penitent during the committee proceedings?'

'Let's say you lose your job here. And then you find yourself applying elsewhere. They will always call us up for a reference check, you know? The senior people will call me.'

I am amazed by the plain delivery of Unni's threat. 'Wow. And I somehow thought companies are impersonal, that they have no time for being vindictive.'

'I guess the question is: is your career more important to you than the ideas – the insipid and vague ideas, I must say – that you have regarding… regarding inevitable evils and technology and dehumanization and all that?'

'As you've suggested earlier, sir, I'm quite good at what I do. I'm quite certain that I'm going to be quite good at things I haven't yet done, too. I will get a job, sooner or later. So, don't threaten me, please.'

Unnikrishnan nods. 'Of course, you will,' he says. 'Then, is it safe to assume you don't regret it?'

I look to my left at the diagram on the glass board. *Do I want to be part of this transformation*? I ask myself. 'You know, maybe telling Vijayalaxmi was an error of judgment. Maybe joining that WhatsApp group was an error of judgment. But these errors don't feel wrong to me. Do you get that? So, fuck this. I think the committee should just fire me. I will quit anyway if you don't.'

'You sure?' asks Unnikrishnan.

'Yes, I am,' I say, feeling a jolt of excitement in my limbs.

'You were going to get promoted this year, you know that? You were going to be the youngest Vice President in BLIC. Probably even the industry.'

'That's good to know. But quitting seems to be the only ethical option to me.'

'Stop talking like a martyr,' says Unnikrishnan. I realize he is scolding me, which is confusing. 'I know you have this silly notion in your head right now. That you're sacrificing your career for a greater idea or whatever. But, mark my words, you'll achieve nothing. And you will be nothing.'

'Frankly, I don't get it. Do you want me to want the job just so that you can feel powerful when you threaten me with termination? I thought you liked simplicity, Unni.'

Unnikrishnan rises from his chair and moves to stand behind it. He takes a deep breath. 'From each according to his ability, to each according to his needs,' he says. 'That's what you want, Mister Saransh Malik. Sadly, we don't deal in those intellectual exercises.'

I study his face for a moment. Unnikrishnan seems devoid of all his charm now. His mannerisms seem vain; his intelligence is boring. This man is not important to me anymore. 'I'm having an epiphany,' I say, feeling emboldened. 'And it tells me that there is a vulgarity in you that Mitesh can never in his life approach.'

I see Unnikrishnan's jaws stiffen.

'Mitesh can't quote Marx to me,' I continue. 'He doesn't know any history other than the stuff he reads on Whatsapp forwards. You offer him a carrot, he is your bunny. He runs where you want him to, squeals when you want him to. You, on the other hand, are the big-picture guy. You made Mitesh because he fits that picture, because in your vision having a lot of bunnies is the most elementary thing.'

'Careful, Saransh,' Unnikrishnan says.

'You said you were curious about me. I would replace the word curious with terrified. What I did terrifies you because it reminds you that the great inevitability can evaporate if smart people begin to empathize with the affected. I'm the blot on your big picture. And you're worried that there may be others. That's why you want to *know* me. That's why this conversation is more important to you than the committee hearings.'

Unnikrishnan starts laughing loudly and artificially and does so for at least a quarter of a minute. Then he plonks himself on his chair, sighing and feigning fatigue.

'Very romantic,' he says. 'I like how you say it – the great inevitability. That's the right way to put it. The empathizers aren't the smart ones, though. The smart ones are those who get on the bandwagon. Now, if you wish to call them vulgar… that's your problem. Usually, I don't like using the term, but since we seem to be talking concepts, let me tell you that this is the fourth industrial revolution. Eighty per cent of human activity is going to be automated in the next two to three decades. Maybe faster than that. For someone with your credentials, and also someone who is likely to be around when all this comes to pass, the answer to the question *which side do you want to be on?* should be very, very straightforward. Unfortunately, you choose to be an outlier. Though I must tell you that you're the *only* outlier at the HO. I talked to Poonam this morning, addressed her misgivings about the underwriting project. Mitesh said it was necessary given your possible deletion from the equation. What did I do? Just laid down the terms: triple bonus, a promotion. She walked out of the room beaming like a highway headlight. She will be implementing the plan you suggested. How does that sound? Let me also tell you that I've been assigned as an advisor to all Bansal group companies for Machine Learning projects. So it's not just BLIC. As a group, we are going to shed a lot of flab in the next twelve months.'

'Why does shedding me involve so much ceremony, then?'

'To ensure you have no avenue to harm the company further. You done with your coffee?'

'Yes.'

'Then you may leave,' he says, his hand pointing towards the door behind me.

I pick up my phone and walk out of the room. Then I turn back, hold the glass door with my right hand, and peer in. 'I just wanted to say one more thing, Unni,' I say.

'Yes?'

'It's enlightening to see a motherfucker from up this close.'

THE NEW DEAL

THE COMMITTEE HEARINGS ARE NOTHING BUT TWO one-hour meetings over two consecutive days. The room they are conducted in is only a few metres away from Zeppelin; midway, in fact, between Zeppelin and the break-out area. Thankfully, I don't bump into Mitesh, Poonam, or the others (George has been terminated) on either day. From the outside I notice that the charts on which the anomaly Post-its had been pasted are no longer present. For a moment, I take this to believe that iBlink has gone belly-up. But I know that isn't happening; the damage has been contained. Though it must be said that the removal of the charts has increased, quite literally, the transparency of Zeppelin. I find myself unable to look in the room's direction for anything longer than a microsecond, but I wonder if the ones sitting inside have had a moment of looking up from their laptop screens and noticing my presence in the office.

During the hearings, the questions posed to me are only about the facts of the matter – which stage was the project in? Did I tell Vijayalaxmi or not? Did I join the WhatsApp group or not? The detail about me having told Jyoti about the project is not brought up – I presume Unnikrishnan didn't want to complicate things by having Mitesh and Mitesh's wife mentioned at the hearings. Not surprisingly, committee-Unnikrishnan shares none of the philosophical curiosity of informal-Unnikrishnan. He speaks sparingly if at all and acts as if he would rather be elsewhere. Only once does he exert his will on the proceedings, though that too is done through proxy and with deniability. This is on the second day when I start stressing my point about giving the LOEs a chance to fit into other roles in BLIC. As I arrive at how this approach could be beneficial to the company in the long run, Unnikrishnan coughs twice and Manpreet, on cue, cuts me off with some minor detail about the WhatsApp group interactions. The manoeuvre brings a wry smile to my face, which Unnikrishnan expertly ignores but Manpreet can't quite help acknowledging by a look of amusement on her face. Towards the end of the hearings, the third person in the committee, Suresh Jain, asks me if I want to continue working for the company. I shake my head to convey the negative. Manpreet then asks me if there is anything else that I want to be taken into consideration. 'Nothing worth your time,' I say in response, after which she asks me to leave the building and instructs me not to resume work until further notice.

A day after the second and final hearing I accompany Jyoti to the Mumbai airport. She's flying to Delhi.

'Until we meet again, if we do,' I say a bit dramatically. We are a few metres from the drop-off curb, right outside the entrance for the departure terminal.

'Start looking for opportunities in Delhi,' Jyoti says, 'your Unnikrishnan will not be able to affect your job search there.'

'That's true for Bangalore, too,' I say.

'OK, Bangalore, then,' she says.

'So it doesn't matter to you?'

'What doesn't matter to me?'

'Why do you have to be so cruel?'

'How am I being cruel?'

'Do you want me to come to Delhi?'

'I do, Saransh. But I don't want to be the person who keeps you from what is best for you.'

'That's so convenient.'

'What? Wanting the best for you?'

'Yes, because it doesn't matter to you whether… whether what-is-best-for-me and what-is-best-for-you intersect or not.'

Jyoti runs her fingers through her hair. 'Saransh, I don't want to argue right now,' she says. 'I've had a great time with you. But not even two full months, right? It would have been ideal if we had more time to make this into something more meaningful. And maybe we will. I hope we do. But please don't put words in my mouth. I like you. But that's where I am at right now.'

I nod.

Jyoti holds my face in her hands and kisses me. 'It is very possible that they will fire me in a month,' she says. 'I'll be back then.'

'Hah.'

'I think I should go inside.'

'OK. Bye, and take care. I'll miss you,' I say.

'Me too,' Jyoti says. Then she moves away from me and enters the departure terminal.

I take a second to let the last two words make me feel slightly better. That Jyoti turns and waves once also helps.

On my cab ride home I try to temper my ego and convince myself that looking for jobs in Delhi – and thereby acting in the hope that Jyoti will eventually love me – would be a good decision. A move to Delhi would also bring me closer to my folks in Muzaffarnagar – just a three-hour drive away. And Delhi has winters.

I open a jobs' website on my phone and scroll through the listings. It is exciting to see all the possibilities – the companies and roles and designations that I could aspire to work in. But after a minute or so a contrary thought begins to grasp me, forcing me to reconsider my white-collared bind to the narrative. Which narrative? The standard narrative of those with my education, my middle-class family, my need for a monthly salary. I will leave this job and then there will be another job where I'm sure another manifestation of the same story will engulf me. There would be peers like Mitesh, desperate to get ahead; there would be seniors like Unnikrishnan, armed with an ideology that can allow anything at all; and there would be projects like iBlink, packaged in abstractions that stimulate the intelligence and make it work against real people with real lives. I look out of the cab window; Mumbai hurries past. Five years, two promotions, hefty increments, bonuses – will I just repeat the cycle in a new city? What would that say about my reasons for doing what I did?

Out of exasperation, or perhaps out of pure whimsy, I speak aloud in Hindi: 'Is there any good way to live in this world?' It becomes a question to the driver.

'Sir?' he asks, surprised.

'Is there a good way to live in this world?' I repeat my question.

'There is, sir,' he says. 'Absolutely, there is. Do your work truthfully. And don't bring harm to others. That's what I do.'

'What if that is not possible?'

In response the driver delivers a lengthy monologue about how what he said is always possible. He gives examples from his own life. I drift off and look outside my window again, this time trying to burn images of Mumbai on my mind. The sun is pouring white gold on glass panels.

A few hours later, the committee decision arrives as an email from Manpreet. It repeats some of what her first email conveyed with updated numbers on the damage that I have caused. Then there is a strange paragraph that points out how BLIC's attrition numbers are the lowest in the industry, how it is among the most preferred employers in the sector, how it had successfully held on to its employees even during the 2009 recession, and so on. The decision is right below that paragraph, in bold. The company intends to put me on a six-month sabbatical during which it shall pay me 60 per cent of my current monthly salary. I was expecting to be fired, so the sabbatical is surprising, but what is even more surprising is the monthly payment – an allowance for doing nothing. The email then delves into a specific scenario: if I were to resign during the sabbatical, the applicable notice period shall be six months, as against the three months that was otherwise applicable to me. Further down, I am reminded of my obligation to keep confidential all matters regarding BLIC for the period of the sabbatical and the subsequent notice period, as and when applicable. Failing this would be seen as a breach of the terms and would invite 'strict legal action.' Finally, the email informs me that I'm expected to come to the office the very next day to accept these terms in person. It needs my signature to be formalized.

I call Jyoti, who must have just landed in Delhi, and tell her about the email.

'What the fuck does that mean?' she says.

'Stay home and get paid,' I say, 'it means the dream is coming true.'

'Don't be silly.'

'If I resign on the last day of the sabbatical, I would be extending it by another six months. So, it is designed to be minimum six months and maximum a year.'

'This isn't generosity, Saransh. It's a jail.'

'Yeah, I know, I know. I'm a bit gobsmacked, though. It doesn't make sense, you know, for an employee who harms his company as gravely as I have not to get fired.'

'Unless there are risks related to firing the employee straightaway,' says Jyoti.

'Yeah, you're right. This is them buying my silence. They are scared. Scared of me talking about it.'

'I guess you've nuisance value right now given the possibility of you talking to the media, and that's what they're paying off by keeping you on a sabbatical.'

'Yeah…'

'So what are you going to do?' Jyoti asks.

'The free-rider in me wants to go with the flow, to accept the money,' I say.

Jyoti goes silent. I was expecting her to laugh at that. 'You there?' I ask.

'Yes… I… I need to catch a cab. We discuss this later?'

'OK, sure.'

I hear a loud explosion and watch the far half of the building collapse as if a chunk of it has been bitten off by a monster of multistoried proportions and all the employees sitting there are getting sucked into the gap that has opened up on our sixth floor workplace; all of them are being sucked away and there is a lot of howling and shouting and I see all the doors of all the cabins fling open and I see Unnikrishnan cartwheeling towards the large hole in the building and out into the void of the world and all the time he shouts 'Transformation Transformation Transformation', and then I see Mitesh somersaulting above the cubicles, sucked by the snafus of the outside world as he shouts 'Sex' with many trailing Xs, and I look around and everyone has disappeared into the void and it is only me and me alone who is unmoved, who doesn't feel any force from the outside world, and what is even more strange is that I am inside my flat, at the little dining table in my living room where I have opened a notebook and have begun to write, for I feel it is the best time to write, with everyone outside, but all that I can write is 'Muzaffarnagar Muzaffarnagar Muzaffarnagar', and it is so strange, so very strange, this thing that I've written, for I can't really read it but still know that it is there, written; and just then Jyoti emerges naked from my bedroom and throws a T-shirt on my notebook and runs outside my flat and I follow her because I don't want her to be seen naked, but in my hurry I trip and stumble down the staircase and I fall and fall and fall and fall…

I wake up. I check the time on my phone. It is close to 2 a.m. No missed call from Jyoti. Last night we talked briefly after she got the cab. She said that I should resign immediately and restrict my BLIC exposure to the three months' notice period that it would entail. She also pointed out that if I accept the sabbatical then no company would hire me because of the long six-month notice period. I blurted out something about the irony of taking work-related advice from her. This irritated her and she said she'd call me back later in the night. 'Hopefully, by then you'd be in the mood to talk about it in practical terms,' she said. With that quip of hers, another layer of irony accreted to my understanding of the situation – a few days ago, it was I who used to ask Jyoti to be practical.

I get out of the bed and go to the kitchen to get myself a glass of cold milk. I think of the dream again. Rethinking the writing bit in it somehow reminds me that I have still not answered Jyoti's email despite promises to the contrary. But what could my answer be now? Haven't I already answered with my actions? In a way, I have been answering her since the day I met her. In a flawed way, of course. Our exchanges usually took the form of a moral compass in a narrative about *me*, about *my* agency, about what I was doing, and what I could do, and what I must have done. Jyoti, the agent Jyoti – the person who could steer her life the way she wanted to with whatever contradictions, hypocrisies, or cruelties that her character could contain – has now begun to reveal itself. And this is what has rattled me. This is what I now misconstrue as irony. This sudden emergence of her story. The dilution of the enigma.

It hits me then that in her story I might just be a minor character.

In the next minute, while sipping cold milk and craving for a cigarette, I shift my thoughts to BLIC, SPG, the project. They are going ahead with iBlink; they will fire the LOEs. I latch on to the sense of defeat this makes me feel and contrast it with the helplessness I felt whenever I thought of Alan Kurdi. The defeat, I find, is bittersweet, sobering;

and it addresses that helplessness, too. *I'm against people losing their livelihoods in the name of progress*. And even though the articulation of this position can be attributed to Jyoti, or to a series of coincidences – from matching with Jyoti on Tinder to giving my number to Vijayalaxmi to visiting Mitesh's apartment for lunch that Sunday – what I did is still my action, what I feel are still my emotions. Automation, or the form in which it will be carried out, will mean automating existing power differentials. The powerful will bask in new-found statistical backing, the powerless will lose ground to inscrutable algorithms.

But who am I in all this? Where do I stand on the power spectrum?

An inchoate answer comes to the fore. I place the half-emptied glass of milk on the bedside table and lie down. Over the next few minutes I feel my body slowly relaxing. I close my eyes, wishing for a dreamless sleep.

In the morning I am woken up by the phone ringing. It is Jyoti.

'I'm sorry, Saransh. I was too tired last night,' she says.

'Yeah, no problem. I went to bed, too.'

'What are you going to do today?'

'I think I'll tell them that I'm not signing the sabbatical letter.'

'That's the right call. But they will try to intimidate you.'

'I'm sure they will. Listen, I have a question.'

'What?'

'Can I...' I pause, thinking how best to put forth the idea.

'Can you what?'

'They've been somewhat worried about your knowledge of the project,' I say. 'Mitesh always thought that was a risk. He'd also told Unnikrishnan, our boss. And now you *are* a journalist. With a magazine that could actually be interested in the story, isn't it?'

'Don't even think about it, Saransh,' Jyoti says. 'The company has denied the project in writing. And what the LOEs say won't count. No magazine will run that story with you being the only source. Even if you find an interested party, and they manage to do a story, imagine what it will mean for you. It will certainly end your career. You'd have to say bye-bye to the idea of working in India forever.'

'No, no, I'm not asking you, or anyone, to actually consider a story.'

'Then what?'

'I'm asking if I can hint at the thing? As leverage.'

Jyoti takes a moment to think about it. 'As a threat, you mean?' she says.

'In a way.'

'My answer is no.'

'Why?'

'Because if your company gets in touch with my magazine, I'd lose my job.'

'How? You could always deny it. You could always say you don't know who Saransh Malik is.'

'It's too much of a risk, Saransh. I'm sure there are other ways for you to avoid the sabbatical.'

'You're missing the point,' I say.

'Am I? What's the point?'

'It's not my sabbatical. I'll push them to drop the project. The LOEs will stay in their jobs.'

A pause.

'It's worth a try,' I add.

'OK,' says Jyoti.

'OK?'

'Yeah, OK. Do it subtly if you can, please. Make sure they're not recording you or anything when you say it.'

'Thanks!'

'Fuck, Saransh. There is a good chance we will both have to free-ride using my father's money.'

'I want to meet Unnikrishnan and Mitesh,' I tell Manpreet.

I'm sitting in the spare chair in her cubicle. I'm dressed informally for the first time inside BLIC HO: a half-sleeved shirt, black jeans, old sneakers. Manpreet is dressed in business formals. The papers for the sabbatical lie in front of me.

'Dude, come on,' says Manpreet in a hushed voice. 'Don't stretch this. Just sign the damn thing. They will pakka let you out after April, once they are done with the project. I'm telling you this informally, of course. You fucked up, you fucked up – fine. Now let the company derisk the way it wants to, na.'

'I want to meet them, Manpreet,' I say. 'I'm not signing anything until I meet them.'

'God knows what keeda you've caught, man. Achcha, Unni told me that you used an expletive the last time you met him. Did you?'

'He had me convinced it was an informal meeting.'

Manpreet laughs. 'Uptight asshole toh he is for sure. No doubts there. Good you gave him a gaali. Now, will you sign the document or will we have more drama? If this were offered to me I'd sign in a flash, I tell you. Saala, imagine, the company giving money to sit at home.'

'I want to meet them.'

'Ugh, man. So stubborn. Fine, I'll go ask Unni.' Manpreet leaves her cubicle and walks towards Unnikrishnan's cabin.

She returns a few minutes later: 'Unni has about twenty minutes before an important meeting starts. He's called Mitesh to his room. You can go.'

I pick up the sabbatical papers and rise from my seat. I see Mitesh walking in the aisle just in front of me. He slows down, looks back and asks, 'What's up with you?'

'Nothing,' I say.

He stops walking so that we are next to each other, and then puts his arm around my shoulder. 'Poonam is doing well with the underwriting project, you know.'

I don't say anything in response.

'Is this about being sorry?' he asks.

'No. About making sorry.'

Mitesh is the first to enter the room with me following closely. Unnikrishnan turns his chair to face us. 'Hi,

Saransh, how're you doing?' he says. Mitesh goes to his side and seats himself on a chair such that I'm facing the two of them across the round table.

'I'm fine, Unni,' I say, seating myself.

'So, what did you want to talk about?' Unnikrishnan asks.

'I want this to be informal,' I say, 'so it would be best if you can show me that there are no recording apps running on your laptop or on your phones. My phone's clear. Look, here.'

Unnikrishnan shuts his laptop and places it inside a drawer. Then the two of them show me their phones.

'You've become quite suspicious, eh, Saransh,' Mitesh says.

'It's not that, Mitesh. Saransh is just doing what I did when he and I last met in this room. When he abused me,' says Unnikrishnan.

I pause a beat, then begin: 'Jyoti, my girlfriend, has found a job with a prominent magazine in Delhi. As a writer of long-form stories. I have a story for her and I have been wondering if she should write it.'

Unnikrishnan and Mitesh look at each other for a moment.

'So you're here to threaten us,' Mitesh says. He shakes his head, imitating disbelief. Unnikrishnan's lips are firmly shut.

'I won't go on sabbatical,' I say, 'so you can keep this with you.' I push the sabbatical papers towards Unnikrishnan. I am deliberately ignoring Mitesh and fixing my gaze on him.

'We don't really need you to sign these papers to actually put you on that sabbatical,' says Unnikrishnan. 'The original contract has enough clauses in it for us to be able to do that. Your signature on this was just an extra precaution, you understand?'

'I want to be released from BLIC immediately,' I say. 'The reason you're letting me go is that I have to move to Delhi for personal reasons. So the committee and its proceedings should be deleted.'

Unnikrishnan narrows his eyes. 'And why should we agree to that?' he asks.

'There is one more thing: I want the LOE project to be dumped,' I say.

'You're seriously the biggest chutiya I've ever met,' Mitesh says. He stands up and starts pacing in the small space beside the glass board on the wall. I see this only from the corner of my eye as I'm still only looking in Unnikrishnan's direction.

'And the fear of the story being published should make us do all these things?' Unnikrishnan asks.

'Yes,' I say.

'You will be the only one speaking in the story, Saransh. Jyoti – that's her name, right – will be risking a lot on you.'

'The LOEs will speak, of course. And I think you've forgotten about George.'

Unnikrishnan shoots a glance towards Mitesh, who takes his seat again.

'You've talked to George about this?' Mitesh asks me.

'Not yet, but I don't think he would have anything to lose if Jyoti approached him,' I say without looking at Mitesh. 'I'm sure he thinks that you guys didn't try hard enough to save him this time.'

'Let's take a step back, Saransh,' Unnikrishnan says. 'I don't know if you read the newspapers. Yesterday there was news of a major IT company laying off 1,000 engineers. Three weeks ago, before any of this mess had begun, there was news of a major real estate developer firing 300 of its employees. You see, these things happen all the time. So what's the story?'

'Come on, Unni, you know that this is different,' I say. 'We're talking about a potential man-versus-machine story here. And the secrecy will make it read like a conspiracy. Imagine: *We reached out to BLIC top management for comment but there was no response.* When an IT company fires engineers, it is responding to macroeconomic considerations... or at least that's what they come out and say. In BLIC's case, we are talking about a secret plan to terminate 10 per cent of the total workforce. No industry pressures, no slowdowns. Just in the name of innovation.'

'These kinds of layoffs will happen everywhere, Saransh, in every industry,' Unnikrishnan says. 'We have talked about this before. I still don't get why you're so emotional about it happening here.'

'Because I think I can stop it here,' I say.

'Why do you think I will be intimated?' Unnikrishnan asks. 'What makes you think I will agree?

'My thinking is simple, Unni. If the story comes out, you'll definitely lose your job,' I say, 'and I don't know whether it will be possible for you to revive your career at this age, especially with this stigma.' I then look towards

Mitesh for the first time since entering the room and say: 'Mitesh will have a better chance, of course.'

Unnikrishnan's mouth develops a hint of a smile. He closes his eyes and leans back in his chair. I've said what I wanted to say. My heart is thumping in my chest. There is silence in the room.

It is Mitesh who, unnerved by Unnikrishnan's inscrutable expression, breaks the silence: 'You were part of the SPG, Saransh. From the beginning. You were involved in everything.'

I choose not to respond to that. Mitesh rises from his chair again and begins to pace around the small space available to him.

Unnikrishnan finally opens his eyes. He joins his hands and leans forward. 'We will release you immediately with the reason you've mentioned,' he says.

'And?' I ask.

'And… fuck off,' Unnikrishnan says.

The thumping in my heart slows down and begins to turn into a sinking feeling. I don't have a repartee. My cards are already on the table, and Unnikrishnan has certainly evaluated the scenarios. 'You sure you've thought about this,' I ask him.

'I've more than five months to shape this story, Saransh. You only have what you know right now. I'm in control here. I can say I'm outsourcing the LOE role. I can even say I'm keeping the LOE role intact and then slowly fill it with minimum-wage dummies. I can cite low performance and start firing LOEs from today onwards. I have countless options. All things considered, my worst case is the layoffs getting delayed by a month or two. You know, I gave you the sabbatical offer to take the risk to zero. That doesn't mean I'm not confident of winning a slightly risky game. If you're smart, which I think you are, you're bluffing right now. But if you and your girlfriend are stupid enough to actually think of doing a story, be assured that we will make you look ridiculous. My advice? Take the deal I'm offering you now and get the fuck out of my room.'

I left Unnikrishnan's room with my mind bereft of ideas and my tail between my legs. Mitesh had rediscovered his grin. But what could I do to stop that grin? I had no other ruse to put forward, no other games to play. I had been bold, of course; I had tried. Perhaps this is how far a fight like this can go.

Walking down the sloping road outside Bansal Tower, I reevaluate the events. I have come out of it all with almost zero professional harm, and in practical terms, that is the best that I could have asked for. I'm free of BLIC. I'm free to look for a job in Delhi. That will require me to make a CV. And in that CV I will have to write about my time in BLIC, I will have to mention how I was a part of the SPG, I will have to mention iBlink. 'Mention' is not the right word, in fact; I will be 'making use' of these things. *Instrumental part of the team that set into motion a machine-learning plan to release significant bandwidth at the branch level. Savings impact expected to be more than ₹15 crores per annum.* In my CV the eventuality of hundreds losing their jobs will be made inconspicuous through jargon. Any future interviewer's eyes will light up at that ₹15 crore figure. He or she will then ask me specific questions about the project: *How did you evaluate your technology partners? What were the challenges you faced?* I will give the right answers. I will narrate the story of the first failure, and of how the second iteration necessitated LOE interviews. The interviewer will be excited even further. He or she will ask me about the methodologies used to codify the qualitative information obtained through interviews. Sensing that I'm close to nailing the job, I will present George's LIFE guide as my brainchild. I'll narrate a couple of LOE interviews as proof that I was right in the thick of things. *Would the prospect of doing a similar project in our company excite you?* the interviewer will then ask me. If I say *No* to that question, the interviewer will ask me *Why?* and I will give some tepid answer about wanting to do something different. I will still be hired, with the interviewer hoping to change my mind later. If I say *Yes*, however, I'll be put in charge of a SPG-like team in the new company. Jyoti will get to be uncomfortable about my job again. But, professionally, it will be a perfect step-up for someone with my experience and my education. Even before the age of thirty, I'll become like Mitesh, with direct access to an Unnikrishnan-like figure. In fact, I might be able to negotiate a salary higher than Mitesh's – sixty lakhs per annum, seventy lakhs even.

As I step into the auto that will take me home, I compare my situation with that of the BLIC LOEs. In April next year when they are asked to leave, all of them will also have to make their CVs. In those documents, they will detail their experience with BLIC. They will mention the transaction volumes they handled during peak seasons, the satisfaction ratings for their respective branches, the commendations they received from others. Interview opportunities will be difficult to come by, though. Their skills will not be valued a lot in the market, for the industry will now know that automating them is possible. During the interviews, when the LOEs talk about the dexterity with which they handled so-and-so exceptional scenario, the interviewer will most likely be distracted. Almost all companies will have copycat projects in the pipeline. In less than a year, LOE-equivalent roles will be wiped out in the entire financial services industry. So even the LOEs who manage to find jobs after April will inevitably lose them a few months later. And there will be thousands of others like them competing for the few scraps that remain. Only a small percentage will be able to learn new skills quickly enough to maintain their lifestyles. The rest will stare down the deep end of a barrel – the same end from which their hard work and occasional ingenuity had, for a few years, lifted them and their families.

The auto arrives at Saibaba Complex. Luckily, I have the exact change needed.